# Home from the Hill

## Susanne Bellamy

Susanne Bellamy

# Dedication:

*For my father, who sailed the Seven Seas*
*And came home*

*"Home is the sailor, home from the sea,*
*"And the hunter, home from the hill."*

*'Requiem' by Robert Louis Stevenson*

Susanne Bellamy

**Prologue**

Graham Peyton squatted and touched the soil around the base of the pole. *Freshly disturbed.* Anger erupted like breath-stealing red and black pain in his head, swirled like a dust storm around him.

*What is a surveyor's marker doing on the slopes of my home?*

Stepping carefully, he scanned the nearby area for more pegs, footprints, any clue about this intruder on his ridge. And while he searched, dread clumped in his gut. When he found the next marker even higher up near his winter campsite, his muscles tensed. Hunkering down, elbows on his knees, he looked out across the lower slope of the ridge, across the creek that gave its name to the town. A band of steel tightened around his chest, squeezed his lungs.

*This is a declaration of war. Someone's trying to steal my home.*

Graham tossed another piece of wood onto the fire, his fireplace little more than the corner remnant of a low stone wall, all that remained of the ruined cottage where he spent the winter months. He sat on a campstool and stretched his feet towards the fire.

Jacqueline appeared on the far side of the clearing, pecking at insects in the leaves. She spied him and ran with her rolling sailor gait straight towards him. Clucking loudly—her chicken version of welcome home, he thought—she fluffed her feathers and strutted around his legs.

Graham picked her up and cradled her in his arms. "Guess you're cold, hey, Jacky? And we're under attack by unknown enemies." He stroked the dark-barred hen's head with one finger. "It's just you and me, Jacky, against whatever malign forces are trying to take over our mountain. The question is, how do we defend ourselves, hmm?"

Jacky clucked, the sound low and soothing as though she understood and sympathised.

Graham stared into the flames heating his dinner. Once upon a time those stones now keeping the wind from his fire had formed the wall of a cottage. He imagined four walls, a door, a window or two . . . he grunted and pushed the image out of his head. Even the thought of walls all around stole his breath. He barely tolerated his tent and that, only when he had to. Like tonight.

He glanced up into the crystal-clear sky. Stars shone like diamond pinpricks in the darkness. "There'll be a heavy frost tonight. Reckon you'll need to sleep inside with me."

Jacky lay in the crook of his arm, her weight insignificant, but her presence warm and comforting. Before young Kaden had entered Graham's life, before he'd stepped up and offered to keep the deaf teenager safe from his underworld uncle, Jacky's company had been enough.

"I wonder how Kaden's doing in his training."

But Jacky failed to reply.

Graham didn't need a reply. He hadn't needed anyone in nearly thirty years, but Kaden's departure had left an unexpected emptiness in his life.

It was too quiet. Lonely.

"Maybe there're more young 'uns like Kaden who need help. Maybe it's time I did something about it. And maybe there's a way to do that and keep people off our mountain at the same time. What do you think?"

Gently he set the sleeping hen into a nest of clothes inside the tent before ladling out a portion of stew onto his tin plate. He ate staring into the flames and thinking. If he could do more work like he had with Kaden, maybe even offer an off-the-grid witness protection service to Jack Donaldson's police friend, Smithy, perhaps they could help keep his mountain free from development?

His mountain and his home, his choice of how he lived his life—they were under attack.

*Unless I do something about it.*

## Chapter 1

Janice Lehman hefted her briefcase into the boot and slammed it shut. Biting winter wind swirled around her ankle boots carrying the chill off southern snowfields and dust from neighbouring paddocks.

"Bye, miss. Have a good weekend." Two of her grade six girls clung to their jackets and beanies as they walked past her.

"Thanks, girls. Are you coming to watch the arrival of the museum building? The truck should be coming in around noon tomorrow."

"Don't know, miss. Tracy might." Shailene stamped her feet, waiting while her friend crouched and tied a loose shoelace.

It was more likely Tracy would be there. Her parents had been involved in the project since the first meeting of the Lark Creek Progress Association when Janice had proposed the relocation of the pioneering museum from nearby Melville to Lark Creek. Setting it up alongside the old Lark Creek schoolhouse on Felix Road would give them two buildings and a decent outdoor area to set up a working forge and other displays.

*I had no idea how much work this would be. What possessed me to volunteer as co-ordinator for that job?*

Overseeing such a big project on top of teaching fulltime

was exhausting.

Wind whipped up more dust and grit. Janice grimaced and closed her eyes against the stinging gusts swirling through the dirt car park behind the primary school. When the wind died down, she opened the driver's door and stepped into her ute.

"Janice, wait up." A deep male voice echoed across the parking area and she halted her headlong Friday afternoon rush to escape school. The voice was familiar, but she had only heard it at the association's planning meetings at the winery, not at work. It was a voice she rather appreciated in its sincerity—*and don't forget appreciating the man who possesses it.*

She climbed out of her car. The wind caught her door and slammed it shut, but her gaze remained riveted on the approaching man.

Graham Peyton. Mid-fifties sat well on his muscled body, his tanned face. Good-looking in a craggy sort of way, still in his prime, from a life lived outdoors.

*The strong, silent type.* A feast for her eyes and better than a drink at the local with colleagues at the end of a long week. "Hi, Graham. What brings you into town?"

"You." His voice was low, the word, innocuous by itself. But coupled with his dark brown gaze and the fact Graham rarely ventured into town, the single syllable heated her cold cheeks.

She gave herself a mental shake. Ridiculous to imagine he was flirting with her. Graham didn't flirt. Heck, the man rarely spoke, to her or anyone else. If he'd come looking for her, it must be something to do with the arrival of the museum building.

"You've found me. How can I help?" She smiled up at him, distracted by a strand of hair blowing across her eyes. Dust, hair, wind cold enough to freeze her eyeballs. She tucked the loose strand behind her ear and scrunched her eyes shut. A sneeze erupted.

"Bless you. Look, I need to talk to you. Can we go somewhere less windy?"

Janice sniffed. Her eyes prickled and a stuffy sensation in her nose boded ill for the weekend.

She looked around the parking area, empty save for her vehicle. Thirty minutes after school finished for the week, what else could she expect?

"No car? I take it you walked down from the ridge?"

He nodded.

"Hop in my car." She settled behind the steering wheel and turned to face Graham as he closed the passenger door. "We can drive up to Bailey's Hotel if you like? Josh will have the fire going in the dining room."

Graham flinched.

Small as the movement was, Janice noticed. Too late, she recalled Graham's son, Rick, telling her about his father's fear of confined spaces.

"Or we could sit here if you prefer?" She sneezed again and

grabbed a tissue from a box in the central console. The box rose with the last tissue and dropped with a light, hollow plink. "'Scuse me."

"Sounds like you're coming down with a cold." Graham's eyebrows angled down and in across his blade of a nose. "I'll shout you a hot toddy at the hotel."

Her mouth formed an O-shape. Surprise stopped her words. *No need.*

That's what she meant to say. No need to put yourself through the agony of a claustrophobe confined indoors. No need to offer a drink to a casual acquaintance because she was coming down with a cold.

"I'd like that, thanks."

Graham seemed more surprised by her acceptance than she was at his suggestion. "Right then." He folded his arms and stared straight ahead.

"The pub it is." She reversed the ute out of her corner parking spot and turned out of the gate towards the main street.

If her head hadn't begun to feel heavy and sniffles to tickle her nose, Janice might have taken pity, taken back her agreement and discussed—*what does he want to discuss?*—in her car.

But the hot toddy was tempting.

Her lips tipped up in a private smile. *Imagine the pair of us sharing a drink by the fireside in the pub.*

The sight of them having a drink, her, a divorced, middle-aged primary school teacher with a man known to be a hermit, would raise eyebrows.

*And won't the talk start.* That was the way of small towns.

But then again, Graham Peyton's appearance in the pub would feed the local gossip mill because his appearance in town was rarer than Halley's comet.

Add a woman into the mix and it would be fun to shock the dyed-in-the-wool regulars out of their winter blues.

Janice parked her ute in front of the hotel and grabbed a small travel pack of tissues from the glovebox. Shoving it into her handbag she turned to find Graham holding her door open.

How long had it been since a man had extended that little courtesy?

*Long before Malcolm and I divorced.* She crushed the slip of memory and smiled at Graham. "Thanks."

He nodded and said no more until she was seated in a chair at the table closest to the freestanding central fireplace. "D'you prefer that hot toddy or something else?"

"A toddy sounds good."

He walked to the serving window that separated the main bar from the dining area, his footsteps soft, his movements, athletic. As he ordered their drinks, his broad shoulders blocked Janice's view of the server. Dark hair with a few threads of silver was pulled back into a neat ponytail tied with a strip of leather.

Broad shoulders and slim hips. She'd always had a thing

for both, but this was the first time she'd really been able to appreciate the combination on Graham.

It was impossible not to watch him. And impossible not to wonder at the trim body beneath his dark-grey trousers and khaki, long-sleeved shirt. Janice's gaze dropped. Graham wore solid boots, worn down at the heel and scuffed, but clean. He'd made an effort with his appearance for this trip into town.

*To see me.*

She'd wondered about Graham Peyton plenty of nights since he'd come down off the ridge last autumn and discovered he had a grownup son. And she'd thought a lot about his quiet bravery when he'd volunteered to keep young Kaden safe and off the grid while the case against his underworld uncle progressed through the courts. The conviction last week meant Ferdy Hickman would no longer pose a threat to his nephew.

Now Graham was back in Lark Creek and wanting to speak with *her*.

Ruing the wind that had messed her hair into wild disorder, she finger-combed it and then applied a quick swipe of lipstick. There was little she could do about her outfit. Practical and streamlined for school activities, it wasn't what she'd have chosen for a drink at the pub, but then, she hadn't dressed for a drink with anyone, let alone a man she liked.

Graham turned from the bar, a drink in each hand and wended his way towards her. Two tables away, Jack Donaldson's legal receptionist, Moira Hughes sat chatting with Bessie Jenkins and Darcy Carmichael, the baker, over glasses of red wine. Darcy glanced from Graham to Janice and gave a surreptitious thumbs-up.

Neither Darcy nor Moira were gossips, but she couldn't say the same for Bessie. Even the hint of a new relationship in Lark Creek would be offered like treasure at her next ladies' morning tea.

Heat rose in Janice's cheeks. *I have only myself to blame for suggesting the pub.* But the thought was less embarrassing than the excitement of sharing a drink with Graham.

"Here. Get that into you." He set a steaming glass in front of her and a nip of neat rum in front of himself and then sat erect, his seat at an angle to the table and his gaze fixed on the window at her back.

*Dad struggles with being indoors*, Rick had told her, but she'd never really associated Graham standing next to the door at meetings of the progress association with his phobia.

He ran a finger inside his collar.

"Is it too hot for you here, Graham? We can move if you like?"

"I'm good."

"Well then, thanks and cheers." She lifted the glass and sniffed. At least she could still smell the scent of hot rum and lemon. The steam tickled her nose. Gratefully she took several small sips before setting the glass on its saucer.

Graham sat erect and still, holding his glass without raising it.

Their gazes met, his flicked away and still he said nothing. She sipped more of the hot toddy, grateful for the slide of heat and lemon over her swelling throat.

"So, what is important enough to bring you into town, and how can I help you?" There, she'd given him a chance to state his visit was about business. But she was sure—*half-sure*—she was wrong.

Still Graham sat, wordless. He gripped his glass, tossed the nip of rum into his mouth and set the glass down. A muscle jumped in his cheek and his gaze darted to the doorway.

Janice heard voices from the far side of the freestanding fireplace, and the scrape of chairs as a group settled in for the afternoon. Closing her eyes she let the hot toddy work its way through her body, warming, relaxing, soothing her. Soon, she would be looking for her bed, desperate to curl up under her doona and close her eyes for the night. With an effort, she opened them.

Graham was watching her, but his mouth remained closed.

Impatience flickered through her. *Maybe the strong silent type isn't so crash hot when it comes to conversation.* Struggling to pin an encouraging smile on her face—the smile she used every day in class with her students—she leaned forward. "Does what you want to talk about have to do with the museum?"

*Please don't let it be that.* But the small chance that Graham wanted to talk business niggled the longer he didn't speak.

"Not the museum. Why, do you need help tomorrow?"

*At last!*

In spite of sniffles and an increasing tightening of her chest, courtesy of her oncoming cold, elation sparked. If Graham's visit today—*and his invitation to have a drink with him*—wasn't about the museum, that only left . . .

She grinned; her smile was sure to tip off Bessie Jenkins that a new romance was blossoming in town. "I think I'll have more helpers than I need when the building arrives, but Fergus Campbell and Rick are going to oversee the initial stages."

"They'll see you right."

"I'm grateful so many people have offered their help tomorrow." Sipping her cooling toddy, she waited for him to reveal his interest and—*what, ask me out?*

Silence stretched again, longer than the elastic loop in an old playground game from her childhood.

Eyes prickling, nose blocked, limbs aching . . . the onset of the cold tested Janice's patience to its limit, even for the man sitting opposite. "Graham, much as I love a guessing game I would appreciate it if you could tell me why you invited me to join you for a drink."

And if that didn't serve to loosen his tongue, she had no idea what to do.

"I was thinking of starting a bush experience group for teenagers like Kaden."

"Teenagers like Kaden?" Sure her expression had frozen in an expectant smile, Janice drew on every ounce of teacher experience she had not to reveal her disappointment.

"Oh, you want to work with hearing-impaired students? I think there are a number of programs already in place for such students." Her gaze darted across the faces of nearby acquaintances, darted to the clock above the servery. The pleasure in being seen with Graham fizzled into nothing, just like every recent grey cloud in the sky. No rain for the region, no date for Janice.

*How could I have misread his intentions so badly?*

Graham leaned towards her and tapped the table with one finger. "I figured that. No, I mean kids who are at risk. Kids who've lost their parents and need to find something meaningful in their lives. Heck, even providing witness protection would be good. I've got the skills." His expression gave little clue to his thoughts. His voice was another matter entirely. It dropped lower and rang with passion and conviction and sincerity.

Graham's voice made Janice take notice, in spite of her woolly head and blurring vision and a whole truckload of embarrassment. At least he couldn't know where her thoughts had been.

But his idea . . .

It lodged in her mind and blossomed like native seeds after a bushfire. "Like a bush-based flexi-school? That's brilliant. Have you talked with anyone about setting it up?"

"No. That's why I wanted to talk to you. How do I start?"

Susanne Bellamy

## Chapter 2

Graham set his clenched hands on the table and focused on Janice Lehman's soft brown eyes. He'd surprised her—that much was evident—but he hoped she'd be agreeable. She had pretty eyes, even if the onset of a cold had rimmed them in red. If he focused on her eyes, he could ignore the walls pressing closer, sliding, gliding, closer and closer and . . .

Janice's mouth opened, closed, and then she frowned. Her gaze darted away, her cheeks turned red and Graham sensed he'd missed something, though what it might be was a mystery.

Staring past her shoulder through the window, he watched small branches whipping wildly back and forth. Wind gusts were increasing. Would the extra tent pegs he'd put in before he came off the ridge be enough to hold his tent? "If you don't know, no problem. I can just—"

Janice's head came up and she met his gaze. The light had gone from her eyes and her smile had vanished, replaced by what he thought of as her teacher face, how he imagined she appeared to students in class.

*Was it something I said?* He searched his memory, trying to remember past the numbing claustrophobia.

Shaking her head and holding up one finger, Janice counted off with her other hand. "First up you need to write a detailed proposal. Purpose, location, costings—all the minutiae beloved by every government department. Then you'll need . . . a—a—achoo!" Janice grabbed a tissue from her handbag and held it over her mouth and nose as a series of sneezes interrupted her explanation. A lone tear ran from the corner of one eye as she blinked and wiped her nose.

"Sorry. Where was I?" In the short time they'd been sitting in front of the fire, her voice had become breathy and nasal. She sniffed, her nose wrinkling with the effort to breathe, and then swallowed. Sucking air through her mouth, she tapped her first finger again. "Okay, so first is your proposal. You'll also need to provide or acquire appropriate accreditation to work with young people."

"I got that before they let me work with Kaden."

"Of course you did." She numbered off a second finger and tapped a third. "There are lots of hoops and bureaucratic red tape to get through if—aah-choo."

Janice closed her eyes and dragged in a noisy breath through her mouth.

In good conscience Graham couldn't keep this meeting going. It wasn't that her red eyes accused him, but she was going downhill faster than a felled tree. "You should go home. I've got a natural remedy back at my camp that'll help with your cold. It will help with your breathing. If you like I could drop it in on my way to—"

"I'll be fine. I'll call into the pharmacy on my way home and pick up some cold and flu capsules. I've got to be on deck tomorrow when the museum building arrives."

"As you wish. Reckon you need to get home and under the blankets more than you need to be explaining regulations to me. Can I see you home?"

"No need. I can give you a lift if you like though. Where are you going?" Was he imagining a chill in her voice? On the drive to the pub she'd sounded interested and pleased by his invitation. Maybe it was simply that she wasn't feeling well. But he wasn't imagining the lack of eye contact.

She didn't want to be here and he was more than happy to get outside where he could breathe. "I'm having dinner with Rick and Gei. You'd be welcome if—"

Janice held up one hand and shook her head. "Not like this. I don't want to spread my germs to your family, Graham. It'll be bad enough going out tomorrow for the arrival of the building. No, I'll buy a mask at the pharmacy and try not to get too close to anyone."

"Fair enough."

"Can I get back to you next week about your idea? That will give me time to look up the department's requirements and put together some information for you." Janice drained her glass.

Truly, she did look under the weather.

A twinge of guilt tugged at Graham. He'd been so focused

on managing his claustrophobia, on not bolting from the table where he sat, he'd barely noticed Janice's rapid decline into a full-blown cold until that last sneeze. "No rush. I appreciate your agreeing to help me."

"Right then. I'll be off home. Will you come into town to watch the building arrive?"

He stood and pushed his chair under the table.

With the promise of release from confinement beckoning, Janice's strange cool behaviour became more apparent.

"Maybe."

Being around more than a few people at a time and his body went into fight-flight mode. Whether it was more flight than fight he didn't want to dwell on. Not when it meant thinking back to the marketplace where the bomb . . .

On every side the walls loomed and wavered and leaned in, trapping him. Jaw clenched, he clamped a lid on the memory.

But he'd made it into town today and he'd managed to stay inside for almost twenty minutes. *That's a step in the right direction, but it's not enough.*

Months ago, he'd come down off the ridge to help Rick and protect the Romney winery and found the son he never knew he had.

From the ridge he'd seen Kaden, penned in the chicken coop and terrified. Unable to turn his back on the orphaned teenager, he'd been drawn into another young man's life. Two weeks ago, Kaden had left to start basic training prior to entering a special program, an Army initiative in inclusivity, and Graham expected to slip back into his old routine. Instead, he didn't know what to do with himself.

Solitude had become loneliness.

Now, the ridge and the life he'd lived there weren't enough. His home was under threat and, for the first time in thirty years, he wanted to do something where interacting with people would be essential. The mere thought was enough to set his heart at battle-readiness.

*I want to help. Just not too many people at once. And not indoors.*

"I imagine you can see most of what happens in town from up on your ridge. It must be like an eagle in its eyrie?" Curiosity brought a warmer note back into Janice's voice.

"Sure. I've seen some funny things and quite a few things that aren't for public airing." He could tell her plenty of stories if he chose.

A flush crept up her cheeks. Janice pushed her chair back and bent to pick up her handbag from the floor. She swayed and her eyes scrunched shut.

Graham gripped her elbow and one hand. "Janice? Are you okay?" *Damn it, the woman is burning up.*

Slowly her eyes opened, and she blinked. "Just a little spinout. I really need to get home and get to bed." Her words slid and slipped and ran together, trying to escape before her mouth caged them.

"I'll drive you." *One hot toddy couldn't be enough to make her slur her words, could it?*

"There's no—"

*Definitely slurred.*

"There's every need. If you spin out while you're driving, you could have an accident."

"Thanks for your concern, but I will be fine." Conflicting emotions chased across her face, settling into a frown. "I—Perhaps I'll see you tomorrow."

He helped her into her coat and then held her elbow as they walked down the hallway and pushed through the double doors onto the veranda. A strong gust of dust-laden wind ripped through nearby trees. Small branches whipped along the footpath. One tumbled across the veranda in front of them.

Janice staggered against him; her shoe caught in the fork of the branch. She gripped his arm and flicked the branch off her foot.

He set an arm across her back and kept her close as they descended the shallow steps to the footpath.

Wind moaned like tormented ghosts around the eaves of the pub and rattled the tin roof like a dog with a bone. "Looks like we'll have a full-on westerly wind by tomorrow. It'll make the trip that much slower for the removal truck, especially coming along the road beyond the ridge."

"Will it slow the trucks down much?"

"Probably."

She pressed a button on her key remote. The car door unlocked with a click and a double flick of indicator lights.

Graham reached for the handle and opened the door for her. "Drive carefully, Janice. I'll—maybe I'll see you tomorrow."

"Maybe." Her smile was dazed, little more than a twitch of her lips and followed by a quick succession of sneezes.

He didn't like letting her drive like that, but she knew her own mind. He closed the door and then watched as she reversed out of the parking space and drove the short distance to Lark Creek Pharmacy before he set off down the footpath towards Leonard Drive and beyond that, along River Road to the winery.

Gei had promised a roast dinner with all the trimmings and Rick was keen for him to taste a new gin recipe for his fledgling enterprise.

As Graham reached the pharmacy, Janice emerged with a paper bag and an open box of tissues clutched in one hand. She pulled several tissues from the box and tossed her purchases into the car before climbing in and slamming the door.

Graham had a couple of good reasons to come into town tomorrow. He'd see the building arrive at close hand, and he'd bring his cold cure in and see how Janice was faring.

*Yes, they're both good reasons to come down off my mountain.*

## Chapter 3

Half the population of Lark Creek was gathered around the perimeter of the site to watch the arrival of the Lark Creek Pioneer Museum building—a former early wooden schoolhouse cut in half and arriving in two loads. Graham looked at the brochure he'd picked up at the front gate on his way into the site. Plans included an interactive tourist attraction on several acres of former school land on the outskirts of town, just beyond the Catholic Church. Plans that were now reaching fruition thanks to Janice Lehman's energy and drive.

Graham looked down the gently sloping block and the familiar tingling began on his scalp, and a band tightened around his lungs, squeezing until each breath was like climbing in the thin air of a high mountain.

He would have seen enough without exposing himself to the tension that filled him in crowded spaces, but an unexpected need to check on Janice had enticed him down off his mountain.

He couldn't see her from where he stood beside Rick's ute, well back from the crowd, but this section of land sloped upwards and gave him a decent overall view of proceedings.

*Close enough.*

The first removal truck pulled up on the single-lane

bitumen road beside Rick and Fergus. As the town's resident builder, Fergus was in charge of construction and Rick had volunteered as second-in-charge. Judging by the pointing and hand gestures, they were giving the driver directions.

The area designated for the building was marked out in blue spray paint on the short bleached grass.

*Like a three-D blueprint.*

Fergus had taken meticulous measurements and a small team of men had set in stumps ready for the building. The stumps stood like soldiers on parade, erect, solid, ready for duty.

The truck began reversing, its high-pitched regular beeps intruding on Graham's flight of fancy.

Rick walked beside the truck, guiding the driver into position. The truck jolted to a stop and air brakes hissed. Soon, the first part of the former schoolhouse was being lowered into position.

Graham's heart swelled with pride. His son was easy to spot over the crowd; as tall as him, with the same dark eyes and square jaw and easy ability to lead others.

The truck stopped and the driver climbed down from the cab and joined Rick who gave him a thumbs-up and patted his shoulder.

Rick might have inherited Graham's looks, but he had his mother's kindness and compassion, her ability to connect with people, and her slow smile. The one she used to give Graham when encouraging him to try something new. The same smile Rick had given him last night when he suggested coming into town and helping him and Fergus set up the building.

*Alice.*

Once upon a time, thinking of Alice—her smile, her strength of character, her love for him—every thought of her had punched out more of his insides because he couldn't be with her. Now, her image was less clear, less certain in his memory, but she lived on in her son.

Graham's eyes prickled and he blinked away unfamiliar tears. Rick had grown into an honourable man despite the poor example of his stepfather.

*A stepfather he would never have had if I'd got my shit together and come back when I should have for Alice and her son. My son.*

He'd been too late to help Alice, too late to reclaim his young bride; but he'd been there to help grown-up Rick, and he'd been there for young Kaden.

It had felt good. Somewhere along the way working with the deaf teenager, Graham had rediscovered part of himself that had been missing far too long.

Up the slope Travis and Katy Roberts strolled, arms around each other, with eyes for no one else.

Had he been that starry-eyed with Alice?

Travis caught Graham's eye and thumbed towards the

clanking chains that were wrapped around the building. "Couldn't resist a close view of the new arrival either, hey, Graham?"

"Rick asked me to help." Graham held out a hand and shook Travis'.

Metal grated and the chains were released, hitting the earth with a heavy thump that rose through the soles of Graham's boots. Dirt puffed up and drifted south on the wind.

"Lovely to see you again, Graham." Katy stepped into his personal space and reached up.

Graham planted his boots and locked his muscles while she kissed his cheek.

"Yeah, nice to see you too."

Rick's Gei had kissed him in the same familiar manner when he arrived for dinner last night. The young ones were all into cheek kissing and touching—arms, shoulders, holding hands.

Invading his personal space.

"All this," Katy spread both hands and encompassed all the activity. "This is our community working together. We're going to do more than survive. We're going to thrive."

Graham nodded. "None of this would be happening if you hadn't set the ball rolling with your B and B."

"True. This woman is one very special lady." Travis kissed Katy's cheek. She turned her head and kissed him, a kiss that showed they had forgotten where they were, forgotten Graham's presence.

A kiss that brought a lump to his throat.

Unbidden, he recalled Alice's adoring expression as she'd gazed into his eyes as they had exchanged their wedding vows in front of a Justice of the Peace.

From this distance, it was hard to remember if they'd been as wrapped in each other as these newlyweds.

A hand touched his arm, pulling him from his memory.

Katy grinned, but a hint of pink coloured her cheeks. "Sorry, Graham. I get so wrapped up in Travis I forget where I am sometimes."

What could he say to that? He understood being in love, and loving Alice had been all consuming. Out of the corner of his eye he spotted Rick approaching and, with something like relief, he turned from the lovebirds.

"Hey, Dad. Glad you came." They shook hands and Rick gave him a one-handed man-hug. "Want to give us a hand before the second half of the building arrives?"

"Sure. I thought it would be here by now."

"Should have been but the driver had to change a tyre." Rick apologised to Travis and Katy. "Sorry to interrupt your conversation, but when I saw Dad, I couldn't let a skilled pair of hands escape. You know how it is." He opened the metal locker fitted onto the tray of his ute.

"No worries, mate. Katy is off to help Janice and her committee set up lunch. I'm about to do the drinks run. Catch you both later." Travis strolled beside Katy, a hand splayed across her lower back, towards an open-sided tent from which came an occasional clank of metal pots. Steam and delicious aromas wafted on the wind.

Rick lifted out a spare tool belt and handed it to Graham and buckled on his own. "Let's get this building settled into its new home."

Half the building sat, one side gaping like a massive wound, empty, and yet so full of promise for Lark Creek. Graham listened while Fergus assigned jobs and then set to completing his task, his thoughts filled with plans of his own.

When he reached the corner stump he straightened, slipped the hammer into its loop on his tool belt and glanced across to the mess tent. Three sides were now covered in canvas that flapped in the gusting wind. Yesterday's conversation with Janice filled his thoughts.

*I should have checked on her when I first got here. Why didn't I just do what I meant to?*

*Because I didn't want to get caught in the crowd down there.*

Disgust filled him. How long could a man allow himself to be governed by fear and not lose the core of his being?

He turned away. The ridge reared out of the land, rising steeply beyond the far side of town. He wished he could be there now, watching the activity from his home and safe place.

*Safe place? Hiding place.*

Struck by the realisation, Graham sagged against the building. *I've been hiding out for nearly thirty years.*

In a daze, he stood back while the second half of the building, which had arrived while they made the first half secure, was set in place.

Fergus called the workers in and checked his watch. "We'll do the second lot of connections after we've eaten."

The small team of workers began an immediate drift towards the mess tent, drawn as though attached by invisible wires to the promise of food.

"Come on, Dad. Grub's up."

*Dad.*

The word carried connection and power and cut through his warping memory. A thrill still ran through Graham at the sound of that name. A choked-up kind of thrill laced with wonder and disbelief at his good fortune.

*This is why I have to pick up the pieces and cobble them together.*

*For Rick.*

Hands fisted in his pockets, Graham walked beside his son into the tent and joined the queue waiting for food. Familiar aromas of Afghani-style curry wafted on the air. Graham's gaze cut to the woman standing on the other side of the long trestle table behind three large pots. Samina held a ladle in each hand and smiled shyly at each person as they held out a bowl for her to fill.

The young Afghani refugee had settled in Lark Creek with her husband and little boy a couple of years ago. She turned to Graham and Rick with a gentle smile. "Gentlemen, take a plate. We have red beef curry and a vegetarian curry, and at the end of the table is dhal and naan bread. Help yourself to them."

Her lilting voice, accented English, even the linen scarf covering her head, caught Graham unprepared. Blind-sided, he was hurled back into the marketplace. Into that tour of duty in Afghanistan.

The marketplace . . .

*The woman's blue head covering flapped in the breeze. Her black hair, visible beneath the dupatta, was parted in the centre. Almond-shaped dark eyes stared into his along the line of his raised rifle. Fear flashed through hers . . .*

His gaze connected with Samina's and his vision cleared.

*This is home. Lark Creek.*

Samina adjusted her dark green headscarf before dipping her head and stirring the nearest pot of curry.

*Green, not blue.*

Rick stepped to one side. "After you, Dad."

*Rick. Lark Creek. Not Afghanistan. I'm not in the marketplace.*

"Dad, are you okay?" Rick's face swam in front of him.

Graham sucked in a deep breath, slowly released it and

nodded. "I'm fine."

Unwilling to reveal he'd zoned into a memory, he focused on how hearing Rick call him 'dad' made him feel. His heartbeat settled into a normal rhythm, but his neck muscles were tight as he held out his plate for Samina to serve lunch. Wisps of memory dispersed, and Graham gave her a tight smile.

*I'm not a soldier. I'm not at war. I'm with my son.*

Samina was simply a young acquaintance and he was Rick's father.

At the end of the serving bench he collected a fork, a scoop of dhal and a piece of naan bread and edged towards the open tent flap looking for a place to eat.

Janice waved him over to where she was sitting near the opening, at the end of a line of chairs borrowed from the school hall. "I wondered if I'd see you today." She patted the chair beside her and then wrapped her hands around a thermos cup. Her voice was husky, and her nose and eyes were red.

"I see you're soldiering on despite your cold." Crumpled tissues poked out of her pocket and a box sat on the ground between her feet.

She touched the mask hanging around her neck with one hand. "I've tried to remember to use this, but it's hard when I sneeze, and when I want to talk to people. Frankly, I'm exhausted."

"Then go home. There are plenty of people here to help."

"But I agreed to oversee this project and—"

"And you have. You've made this happen. But you don't have to stay and connect the parts of the building. You don't have to oversee the tightening of every nut and bolt, or the serving of lunch. Good people are here to contribute their skills today thanks to the work you've done. Why not go home and rest now?"

"I need to stay and—"

"You've given everyone directions, haven't you?" An edge of acute discomfort sharpened his voice. It happened whenever more than a couple of people were near, but Janice didn't deserve to be on the receiving end of his phobia. With conscious effort, he dialled back the gruffness. "They know their jobs?"

"Yes."

"So, let them carry out their jobs. Trust them."

She closed her eyes and buried her nose in the steam rising from her mug of tea. When she opened her eyes again, he saw a glimmer of moisture before she blinked and sniffed. "I couldn't ask for better help than what's been freely given here today. You're right. I'll be better off at home instead of risking spreading this wretched cold." She stood, staggered. Her hand grasped thin air.

In one swift movement Graham set his plate down, stood and gripped her elbows. "Are you okay?"

"Head spin." Her fingers dug into his arms.

"That's the second time. This happened yesterday too. How

about I drive you home?"

Her head hung as if she lacked the strength to hold it upright, and her breathing rasped as though she'd run a marathon. "If you wouldn't mind, thanks." She dug into the pocket of her coat and held out a set of keys.

He took them but kept an arm around her waist. "I'll tell someone to tell Rick I'm taking you home and then we'll get out of here."

They walked slowly towards her car parked near the packed dirt driveway onto the site and he opened the passenger door. The trailing end of her coat belt slipped down, dangling almost to the ground. He grabbed it, handing it to her without a word. Her fingers brushed his as she took the belt. They were hot, her cheeks were two bright spots of colour and her forehead glistened with sweat.

Graham climbed into the driver's seat. It was obvious Janice was running a temperature, and a fair bet that by tomorrow she'd be unable to get up let alone supervise anything at the building site.

"Can you stop at the chemist please? I need some sort of eucalyptus rub and more tissues." Her voice was little more than a croak and her eyes closed as she spoke.

"Sure." A short drive down Main Street, he pulled into a parking space right in front of the pharmacy.

She took a ten-dollar note from her pocket and handed it to

him. "Let me know if it's more than that."

"Won't be a minute."

When he returned with a paper bag and a three-box special of tissues, Janice was slumped in the seat, her head resting against the side window and her breathing, noisy and slow.

*Slow enough that she's asleep?* "Janice?"

"Mmm . . ."

As gently as he could, Graham reversed out of the space and drove the couple of kilometres to Janice's home. The lowset brick house on an acre just south of town had all the charm of a red-bellied black snake, in spite of Janice's attempts to cultivate a garden in the front yard. Bland, boring sixties red-brick, the house squatted on the block like a malevolent gnome.

He pulled up under a utilitarian metal carport, switched off the engine and turned to his passenger. "You're home. Janice?"

Her eyelids opened slowly, heavy and swollen. "Oh, good. Thanks." She fumbled with her seatbelt, unclipping it.

Graham strode around the car, opened the passenger door and offered his hand.

Seeming surprised by his courtesy, she lifted hers with what seemed like a conscious effort and set it down in his. Her skin was damp and hot.

"You're burning up."

"Like a comet? How about that." She climbed out and sagged against the car. "I don't feel good."

"Which of these is your house key?"

"The blue one." Her head dropped back against the car.

Graham flicked the blue key up and then, without asking, put her arm around his neck and picked her up. His fingers dug into several layers of clothes, but she hung limp in his arms.

"What are you doing?"

Idle curiosity tinged her tone, rather than any hint of outrage. It was a measure of how ill Janice really was that she didn't protest. He wouldn't have dared such an intimacy if she'd been well.

"Taking you inside." He carried her to the front door and set her down while he unlocked it, and then scooped her up again and carried her inside. "Where's your bedroom?"

Her head flopped onto his shoulder, but she lifted a hand and pointed vaguely towards a short hallway. "That way."

Through an open doorway he spied a geometric-patterned bedspread in shades of gold and deep blue. A small pile of neatly stacked books sat beside a box of tissues and an expensive looking lamp. A pair of purple woolly slippers peeked out from under the bedside table. Janice's bedroom looked warm and restful—*like her*.

He sat her on the bed and eased her coat from her shoulders. "There you go. You get comfortable and I'll get the rest of your gear from the car."

"Thanks."

By the time he returned with her handbag and the bag from the pharmacy, Janice had curled up on top of her doona and was sound asleep. He pulled the doona out from beneath her, slipped off her shoes and then pulled the doona up to her chin. A hunt through her kitchen cupboards rewarded him with a glass and a water jug. He filled both and set them on the bedside table and turned on the lamp to its softest setting.

What else could he do for her? Was there someone he could call to check in on her? Family? Friends? He had no idea where to begin, but concern about her rapid deterioration made him hesitant to leave her alone. "Janice?"

She was unresponsive and Graham was left feeling uncharacteristically at a loss about what he should do.

Living on the ridge, he had no one to worry about, or to look out for. With the exception of Kaden, it had been too long since he'd had the right to feel responsible for anyone other than himself.

*All of my son's life when I should have been there for him.*

He'd been sent to fight another country's war and returned a shadow of his former self—a man so changed he'd been too afraid to return to his wife, or the son he hadn't known about. In a very real sense, the husband Alice had sent to war had never come home.

Regret and sorrow tugged at Graham.

The army had told Alice he was MIA, presumed dead.

Believing them, she'd disappeared from the small apartment they'd set up home in.

All those years when he should have been taking care of his wife and child, and he hadn't.

He had no right and no responsibility for Janice either, aside from his concern for a fellow human being who was ill.

Through the window of her bedroom he could see O'Reilly's Ridge rising sharply to the twin turrets at its peak. His spirit lifted at the thought of his campsite awaiting his return, but he couldn't erase the spike of guilt at the idea of leaving a sick woman to fend for herself.

"Janice? I'm going back to the museum, but I'll call in and check on you on my way home. Is that okay?"

"Mmm."

Should he take that as agreement?

It was probably all the response he was going to get.

"Take my car." Her voice was muffled by the doona and her cold, but her intent was clear. Maybe she'd be glad that someone was checking on her.

Leaving the bedroom door slightly ajar, he switched on a lamp in the loungeroom in readiness for his return and locked the door behind him. Coming back to check on Janice was the least he could do. It was the right thing to do, until he could find a more suitable person.

Strange dreams spun through Janice's mind. She floated through space in a spaceship with Graham Peyton at the wheel. He reached across and stroked her hair. "Where would you like to go next? Mars, or into the outer galaxy? I've made chicken soup and wattle-seed cake." His hand was warm on her forehead and she turned into his touch.

"Fly me to the stars. Show me the universe."

*How she longed to escape this small world; the smallness of her life. Had it always been so small or—*

"I'm going to lift you up so you can take some tablets. Ready?"

Janice kept her eyes closed. Graham had such a lovely voice, deep and comforting and reassuring. Like he knew what he was doing and would take care of her. It was nice to be taken care of.

Once, she'd had someone who'd cared about her.

But Malcolm had stopped caring; stopped loving her; stopped everything and divorced her.

An arm slid around her shoulders and another pillow was added behind her back.

"Open your eyes for me." *Why am I hearing Graham's voice and not Malcolm's?*

She didn't want to open her eyes. She didn't want to let go of this very nice dream and discover she was alone again, with a throbbing headache and aching muscles.

Of course it was impossible that either man could be here in her home, in her bedroom. But still . . . the dream of Graham was nice.

Cool glass touched her lower lip. With more effort than she thought possible, she forced her eyes to open.

In the soft light of her Tiffany bed lamp, Graham's face swam in front of her. She blinked, slowly.

He tipped the glass and cool, delicious water spilled into her mouth. "Just try to drink a little more and then see if you can swallow these tablets."

"Are you actually here or am I dreaming?" Her voice cracked and she coughed, the action wracking her body, sending sharp pains through her head and daggers digging into her throat.

"I said I'd come back after we finished setting up the museum building to check on you. You've got one helluva temperature. I'm not sure that hospital wouldn't be a better place for you."

"No hospital. I'll be fine."

"You're not fine, woman. You're sick. There's cold and flu tablets here that you haven't opened. Do you think you can swallow them? Otherwise I'll crush them for you." His no-nonsense tone was so like hers when dealing with a difficult student; a tone that said he knew he was right; a tone that brooked no opposition, but it felt weird to have it turned on her.

She tried swallowing saliva. Pain raced to both her ears.

"I'll manage."

He checked the dosage and popped two night tablets into her hand. "Do you prefer water first, or after you've got the tablets in your mouth?"

"After." She raised her hand and tipped the pink discs onto her tongue.

Graham held the glass to her mouth.

With a shaking hand she controlled the flow, gagging a little as tablets and water fought their way past her swollen throat.

"Good. Now, is there anything you want, need?"

"You're going? Of course you're going. Sorry." She closed her eyes and sank back into the pillows. The night had taken on a surreal quality.

She knew she was in her home, in her own bed, but, oh, how nice it was to have Graham here to look after her.

*It's been so long since anyone cared.*

Not that she needed anyone to . . . to . . .

Tender hands tucked the doona beneath her chin and the light was turned down low.

No, she didn't need anyone to look after her . . . But it *was* nice.

## Chapter 4

"Knock, knock, good morning."

Janice woke with a start, her eyelashes glued together with sleep and whatever ailed her. Maybe she was sicker than she'd thought when she briefly surfaced in the dawn light and staggered into her ensuite. She must be dreaming again because that greeting was Graham's voice, even though she was sure she was awake.

A warm, callused hand settled lightly on her forehead and she forced her sticky eyelashes to open. Graham came into bleary focus.

"You're still hot, but maybe not quite as bad as last night."

Graham was definitely here in the flesh, in her bedroom and feeling her forehead. *Talk about wish fulfilment.*

*Water.* The words jiggled in her head and Janice tried to moisten her dry mouth. "Water please." Was that wimpy croak of a voice hers?

Graham half-filled her water glass and offered it to her. "Can you manage like that or do you want a hand to sit up?"

"I think I can manage." Her body ached and the room spun as she struggled to sit up. "I'm as weak as a baby."

"Given how high your temperature spiked last night I'm not surprised."

"Last night? How do you know that?"

"I slept on the couch. Came in to check on you every couple of hours." He plumped up a spare pillow and carefully tucked it in behind her. "Better?"

"Much, thank you. I don't remember you being here." And that both worried and fascinated her. Graham had slept the night in her house because he was worried about her. Not many friends would do that, let alone those who were little more than an acquaintance. "That was kind of you."

"A temperature like you had could easily have turned nasty. It peaked around three this morning. Reckon you were delirious." His gaze flicked away. Standing beside her bed, he had a quality of stillness and strength and dependability that was very appealing, very—

*Delirious? What did I do?*

A strange sensation fluttered in her stomach. "Did I—say anything odd?" Remnants of strange dreams flickered through her mind. If she'd voiced any of that to Graham, she'd be mortified.

"Not really. You were away with the gumnut fairies. Do you think you could eat something, some soup maybe?" Gruff dismissal—redirection. Was that his way of getting past an awkward moment?

She needed the bathroom and privacy. She needed a few moments alone, moments to recover from her surprise and probable embarrassment before she spoke with Graham again. She really needed to know she hadn't revealed her little fantasy trip to the stars.

But it could wait until she'd fortified herself with time and hot soup. "I'll try a little soup please."

Tossing the doona off took all her strength; it was harder than hefting rocks in her garden. Her arm felt like a lump of lead and her fingers lacked the ability to keep a grip on even a corner.

"Where do you think you're going?" Graham's hands settled on her shoulders and applied a light pressure.

"I need the bathroom."

Graham's hold changed and before she knew it, she was on her feet, his arm around her waist and shuffling towards her ensuite.

"Do you want me to wait for—"

"Please don't. I'll be fine." *Please let me be fine.* "I think there's still a tin of tomato soup in the pantry." She closed the door, her legs trembling with the effort of standing. Supporting herself on the wall, she edged towards the sink and leaned heavily on the vanity unit.

It was so kind of Graham to have stayed the night to keep an eye on her, but she needed him to leave before she really made a fool of herself and babbled out some delirious dream. Or some absurd fantasy.

*How soon can I get him to leave?*

Graham poured a small serve of his homemade soup into a saucepan and set it on the gas stove to heat. He capped the pottery jug and returned it to the fridge. Keeping an ear out for movement from the bedroom and stirring the soup every so often wasn't enough to stop him thinking about Janice's fever during the early hours of morning.

*Fever dreams*, he remembered his mother calling them when his twin brother had fallen ill. Thomas had caught a chill during a primary school camp and spent a night moaning about giant spiders chasing him through the bushes and up the mountain.

*"Tom isn't afraid of anything, Mum. Why is he going on about spiders?"*

Mum had hugged him to her, the scent of lavender and eucalyptus oil pleasant and reassuring. *"I suspect Tom might have arachnophobia—that's a fear of spiders, sweetheart. And he's hidden it all this time. People often say things when they're feverish that they'd never reveal in their right state of mind."*

Was that what Janice's *"Fly me to the moon"* comment was? A peek into her desire for something more than what her life in Lark Creek offered? Or was it no more than a weird dream brought on by the medication? He stirred the soup and then dipped a spoon in, lifting it to his mouth. A little more warming, but not too hot and he'd try serving it to Janice in a cup.

The water pipes groaned, rattled, followed by the snick of the ensuite door being opened. He turned the gas flame to its lowest setting before heading down the hall into her bedroom. "Okay, Janice? Soup's nearly ready."

She was leaning against the wall, her hands white-knuckled where she gripped the doorjamb and her eyes, closed.

Graham slipped an arm around her waist.

She sucked in a breath through her mouth and he was almost certain there was a rattle in her chest.

"Back to bed with you. I've got you." His hand settled on her waist above the flare of hip. Soft and warm, with the slightly sweaty scent of a body too long between the sheets. It had been a long time since he'd encountered it. A long time since Alice had tempted him to spend a whole morning in bed.

He eased Janice onto the bed and settled her onto the bank of pillows before pulling the doona up to her chest. For God's sake, Janice was sick and needed his help. He stepped away quickly, unable to stem the inappropriate thoughts. "I'll be back with the soup."

*Inappropriate and surprising and strangely—welcome.* Maybe his ability to connect with people—*some people at least—* hadn't died with Alice.

He checked the temperature of the soup and poured it into a thick mug. Fresh bush aromas wafted in the steam. If Janice had a simple cold, this bush remedy would help, but he was concerned about that rattling cough. Mug in hand, he walked the short distance to her door. Maybe he would stay on her couch again tonight—just to be sure.

He pushed the door wide and set the mug down on the bedside table.

Janice smiled up at him. Soft light from the lamp highlighted a few silver strands in her chestnut brown hair. A twenty-year-old memory superimposed itself, a memory viewed from the heights of the ridge—of a young and smiling Janice leaving the Catholic Church on the arm of her new husband. Since then, her husband had left her and Lark Creek, but Janice had chosen to stay.

Funny how he remembered her smile. It hadn't changed.

"Try to drink a few mouthfuls. It's homemade and full of lots of good foods from the bush."

Janice picked up the mug and flicked a searching look at him. "Did you make this?"

"Yes."

She held the mug beneath her nose and sniffed. "I can't smell anything. What's in it?"

"Family secret. Go on, try it. It shouldn't be too hot."

Cautiously she sipped the soup. "I wish I could smell it even if I can't taste it, but my tastebuds have gone walkabout. I couldn't smell a bushfire if it was right behind me."

"I'll make more when you're better. You'll like the flavours in it."

Words he'd never offered to anyone emerged unbidden.

Words that held a promise. Words that were a commitment of sorts.

To deliver on his promise he would have to leave the ridge and come back into town. His stomach flipped, dived, clenched.

*I'll make more for you when you're better . . . Where had that come from?*

## Chapter 5

Gravel crunched and a vehicle turned into Janice's driveway. Hers was the last house on the dead-end road. Unless someone took a wrong turn there was no passing traffic. Graham lowered the newspaper he was reading, folded it in half and set it down on the back porch. Maybe one of her friends had come looking for her.

He walked down the side of the house. Rick's work ute pulled up behind Janice's, the diesel engine chugging to a standstill. His son got out of the car and strolled down the red concrete path towards the front door.

Surprised but pleased to see Rick, Graham brushed past one of Janice's feathery pot plants with a rustling sound he was more used to hearing down near the creek. The vibrant green softened the overwhelming red of brick walls, concrete veranda and path.

Rick offered his hand. "Hey, Dad. I saw you driving Janice's car away from the museum site. What are you doing here?" Rick leaned against a metal upright and folded his arms.

"Morning, son." Graham sat on the top step and Rick sat on the next one down. The westerly wind wasn't a problem on the east-facing slope of the ridge. Here on Janice's exposed block, it leached the warmth from her house faster than water down a drain, but the morning sun felt good on his skin. "Janice is ill. She all but fainted—twice. I thought someone needed to keep an eye on her."

"And you volunteered for the job?" His son's eyes narrowed beneath a silent frown.

"Someone had to. Her temperature spiked. Over a hundred, she was. What else could I do but stay?"

"Dad, you almost never come into town. I had to twist your arm to get you off your mountain to help with the museum, and here you are, in town, three days in a row." He chuckled. "Who are you and what have you done with my father?" The jovial tone didn't disguise Rick's curiosity.

"I didn't know who to call. Janice refused to go to hospital."

"Seriously, you could have called me. Gei or her mother would have been over like a shot. I can call her now and get her to relieve you if—"

Graham's hand shot out as though with a mind of its own. He didn't give even a passing thought to the reason as he caught Rick's wrist. "It's fine. I've brought her some of my soup. Seems to be helping."

"And what about at night? What if she takes a turn for the worse?"

"I'll hear her." Heat rose up his neck with the admission. *Not that I've done anything to feel embarrassed about, but will Rick see it the same way?* "I've slept on her couch the last two nights."

"You've—inside?" The stunned tone of Rick's *inside* rose like a cresting wave.

It towered over Graham with all the power of indignation and disbelief. It questioned and demanded to know if his *phobia* was exaggerated—or, God forbid, a lie.

"I might not have heard her if I'd slept outside."

Rick turned away and ran a hand through his hair. When he turned back his gaze pinned Graham. "You refuse to stay over and sleep in our home. You tell me you hate being inside for more than the length of dinner and even that is a strain."

"I don't like being in—"

"Even though the temperature was barely above freezing we had coffee on the veranda after dinner the other night because you prefer being outside. I don't get why suddenly you're okay with sleeping in a room."

Graham shook his head, marvelling as realisation dawned. "Neither do I. Closing Janice's front door and shutting the outside out *is* difficult; there's no denying it. But staying was the right thing to do."

Only now that Rick had voiced it, named it and made him think about it, his lungs constricted, squeezing all the air out like he was a deflating balloon. He gazed at the hills, followed the line of them to the ridge. *His* ridge.

"I left the curtains open and cracked a window, enough to feel the wind but not lose the warmth inside. And each time after I check on Janice, I go for a walk outside. Seems to help."

Rick sucked in a deep breath and frowned before a smile—*is that weird stretch of his lips a smile?*—replaced it. He nodded, shook his head and finally let his gaze meet his father's. "Sounds like some sort of therapy, but I'm no expert. Good for you."

"There's nothing therapeutic about it. Janice needed help. I was the only one around. End of story."

*I could have tapped one of the women in the mess tent to take Janice home. Why didn't I?*

That was another thing he hadn't thought about at the time. Didn't want to think about now. "Don't make more of it than there is. Any decent person would have done the same."

"That's true—ah, that's great, Dad. Look, if things change and you need help looking after Janice, give me or Gei a call."

"Yeah, will do."

"And Dad?" Rick pulled him into a man-hug and thumped his back. "Well done."

Graham leaned against the veranda post watching until Rick's ute disappeared over the crest of the road and turned his attention to the distant hills beyond his ridge. A blue haze cloaked the slopes except for a broad slash of brown from which rose silvery pylons, arms raised like praying giants.

He closed the door with more force than he'd intended and stood, hand on the doorknob, listening. Had he disturbed Janice with that slam? When there was no response from her, he crossed to the bookshelves and browsed her library. Teaching textbooks filled the lower shelves, but the upper shelves surprised him. Travel, action adventures, crime—her tastes in reading reminded him of her 'fly me to the stars comment'. Maybe his mother had been right about fever dreams revealing the real person.

He pulled out a John Grisham novel and dropped onto the sofa. He'd had enough of distant places to last a lifetime.

Janice rolled onto her back and sifted through the bits of conversation she'd heard. *It wasn't like I was trying to overhear.* But both Graham and his son had voices that carried, commanding voices that marked them as men others would follow. Did follow, from what she'd seen of both of them since Rick's release from prison.

Rick had told her about his father's claustrophobia, and she'd caught a sense of its effects at the handful of community meetings Rick had persuaded his father to attend. Graham never moved far from the door and if he sat, it was always next to the floor to ceiling windows, but he attended. Such was the power of a father's love.

*Why, but more importantly, how is he still here looking after me if he can't bear to be inside for long?*

She pushed the doona down and eased her legs over the side of the bed, testing her strength. When she was confident of going to the bathroom without falling over, she stood. Her feet touched her slippers right where Graham had set them the last time he'd helped her to the bathroom. *How embarrassing.*

Memory was a slippery thing. Her practical self knew he was just doing what needed to be done helping her in her weakened state to get to the bathroom, but in her memory Graham's arm around her waist and the strength of him, the very solidity of his presence, had reassured her that he cared.

But he was just a friend.

*Little more than an acquaintance really, regardless of his kindness.*

The man she admired—*with the occasional lustful dreams about him*—had done what any decent person would for someone who lived alone. The same as her friends would have done if they'd been the ones with her when she took ill. And now she was on the mend—was she on the mend?—Graham would soon head off back to his home on the ridge.

It hadn't occurred to her before but now she wondered where on the ridge he lived. Did he own land up there? Had he built a cabin among the eucalyptus trees?

She wriggled her feet into her slippers and stood, one hand gripping the bedhead for balance.

*Can a claustrophobe live in a cabin?*

## Chapter 6

The bedside lamp softened the darkness of evening and Janice's stomach rumbled as she opened her bedroom door. She steadied herself on the wall of the hall and headed towards the light in the loungeroom.

Graham sat within a circle of light from the floor lamp at the far end of the sofa next to a slightly open window. She had a single second to register the image before he was on his feet, the book closed around a finger.

"Sorry, did you call for me? I didn't hear you." He held the book out and shrugged. "It's been a long time since I've got lost in a book."

She glanced at the cover. "That's a good one. It's one of my favourites."

"Yeah, it's good." He glanced at his watch, an old analogue on a leather strap that had seen better days a decade ago. "Are you hungry? It's nearly dinnertime."

"A little. Can I get you something?"

"You take a seat. I made a stew with lots of vegetables. Help you build up your strength again."

"You made it? Of course you did. You made soup for me too, didn't you? Or did I dream that?"

"You've drunk most of it, but there's one more serving for tomorrow if you want it." He disappeared into the kitchen.

Plates clattered and she imagined she caught the hint of chilli.

Malcolm had never made a meal for her, even when she'd been late home from meetings or snowed under with school reports. On those nights he'd eaten at the pub and she'd more often than not had baked beans on toast. But she'd loved her city-born husband, with all her country girl's heart; loved him as they tried to make a family; loved him until the day he walked out and broke her heart.

"Do you want to eat at the table or are you comfortable there on the sofa?" Graham held a steaming bowl and soup spoon in each hand.

Janice blinked to clear her vision. It was just sleep grit in her eyes, she told herself, and she shouldn't make more of Graham's gesture than it was. He was a friend—*we're past being acquaintances now*—looking after her. "Let's sit at the table."

While he set the bowls on her dining table and pulled out a chair for her, Janice shuffled slowly across the open plan room. "I feel like a little old lady aching in every bone." She sat with a barely suppressed groan.

"Not up to dancing the night away just yet, hey?" He offered a basket of rough-ripped bread.

"Maybe not for a night or two." She took the smallest piece

of bread and set it on the wide flat rim of the soup bowl. "Do you know how the museum installation is going? I feel bad for not asking earlier."

Being weakened by illness had changed her priorities. She'd barely been aware of Graham in her house over the past couple of days. His presence belonged to a dream state and the world beyond her bedroom ceased to exist as she floated on a sea of medication and strange dreams.

"Rick said the main building is at lock up stage. There'll be another working bee over the coming weekends to paint and gussy up the interior and then your committee will be able to start filling the display cabinets."

Her head ached at the thought of diving back into work, and the dozens of little decisions she'd be required to make. "I look forward to getting the museum up and running."

"You won't be able to start for a month; maybe two. Reckon that isn't a bad thing. You need to take it easy for a bit."

"Do I look like I've had the stuffing knocked out of me?" She smiled, but the implication behind his words was clear. "I must look a fright?"

Her hand crept up and tucked a lank lock of hair behind her ear. Could he see the tremor in her fingers? Quickly she dropped her hand into her lap.

"Yeah."

That stung, even though she knew it to be true. Graham

called it as it was and what business did she have to take his comment to heart? Friends told each other the truth. *But still . . .*

She looked down at her meal, picked up her spoon and slowly sifted through until she found a small piece of pumpkin.

"Sorry. Guess that wasn't tactful." Graham cleared his throat and dug his spoon into his bowl. For the next few minutes only the scrape of spoons on china passed between them.

When she was finished eating, Janice set the spoon in her bowl and pushed her chair back from the table. "Thank you for the meal. It was delicious."

"Not too much chilli? I didn't know if you liked it or not."

She'd tasted a hint of chilli, but any subtle flavours had been lost on her. "Anything someone else cooks always tastes better. Now, if you'll excuse me, I'm off to shower and then bed."

Graham stood and stacked her bowl inside his. "I'll be nearby—"

Wrapping her shredded dignity around her, Janice held the back of her chair and drew herself up as straight as she could. "I'll be fine thanks, Graham. I'm on the mend now, but I really appreciate all that you've done for me. When I'm a bit more myself you'll have to come over for a meal so I can thank you properly."

"I'd like that." With a nod, his gaze slid away before he headed into the kitchen.

The last thing she heard before she closed her bedroom

door was the swish of water in the kitchen sink.

Susanne Bellamy

## Chapter 7

Graham had washed and dried the dishes and was putting Janice's slow cooker away when he heard the crunch of tyres on the gravel driveway. A car door slammed, and the security light switched on before footsteps climbed the front steps.

A cheery rat-a-tat-tat echoed through the loungeroom.

Graham opened the front door, bracing himself for Gei's familiar peck on his cheek. A man stood there, his back to the door and hands in his pockets. A baseball cap sat on short-back-and-sides. The security light picked up silver in a pair of token sideburns.

He turned, met Graham's gaze, and the smile on his face faltered.

"What are you doing in Janice's house?" Suspicion, worry, dislike—the series of negative reactions flickered across Malcolm Lehman's face in quick succession.

Graham folded his arms and leaned against the doorjamb, casually blocking the doorway against the unwelcome visitor. "What are you doing back in Lark Creek is a better question."

"None of your business. Where's Janice?"

Graham wasn't pleased.

*But maybe Janice will be pleased to see him?*

Not that it was any of his business if Janice was in touch

with her ex-husband, but the man had left her broken-hearted. Even living high on the ridge Graham knew what the townsfolk said, what Gei and her mother had let slip, and what he'd seen through his binoculars. Broken-hearted and empty, they said, until several months later, she became resigned to her loss.

Snippets of overheard conversation between Gei and Katy Roberts at the first meeting of the progress association filtered into his mind.

*Louse*, was Gei's name for the man who'd left his wife because she couldn't have his children.

Graham thought about that meeting where Katy had set out her plan to turn her grandmother's home into a B and B, and asked for community input. Janice had jumped at the chance to oversee the pioneer museum project.

*My contribution to the revitalisation of Lark Creek*, she called it.

*Her salvation*. Graham kept the thought to himself, but she'd blossomed since taking on the museum project.

*Now the bastard is back and I'm acting like I've a right to protect Janice from him. But does she want my protection?*

Lehman peered past Graham's shoulder. "It's no concern of yours why I'm visiting my wife."

"Ex-wife. You divorced her, remember."

"Still none of your business. Where is she?" Lehman took a step as though he would push past.

Graham moved, enough to block the doorway completely. "Gone to bed. I was just washing up the dinner things."

Graham grinned. A man who left his wife as Lehman had left Janice deserved no quarter.

"I'll tell her you called." He gripped the edge of the door and stepped into the room ready to close it on Lehman.

"Graham, who is it?" That quaver was back in Janice's voice. It sounded thin and reedy.

*And worried? Or is that quaver hopeful?*

Graham couldn't tell. He didn't know Janice and her hopes well enough to be able to tell. *I'm out of practice with women in general.*

He swung the door wide again and stepped through the doorway, forcing Malcolm to take a step back, before turning to Janice. "It's Malcolm."

*It wasn't my imagination. I didn't conjure him from the pit of misery he left me in.*

Here he was, back in Lark Creek. It could only be to see her . . .

*And didn't I think the same thing when Graham showed up the other day?*

*Once bitten.* Tamping down the confused mix of emotions, she allowed a slight softening of her mouth. Not a full smile. Malcolm didn't deserve that. Not after leaving her a blithering mess. Not after he'd made a mockery of their wedding vows.

*Why is he here? To see me?*

"Hello, Malcolm."

"Hello, darling. May I come in?" Malcolm stepped forward, seeming confident of his welcome.

Graham stood to one side, his arms folded across his chest. His face was hard, expressionless, but that look in his eyes . . .

If eyes were the windows to the soul, she feared for his. That look reminded her Graham had been a soldier. He'd killed men in the line of duty. And the laser-look he sent Malcolm should have blasted him into tiny pieces. Janice shivered.

Graham stepped past Malcolm and stood at her side. "Your call. I can send him packing or put the kettle on, but you need to stay in the warmth."

Should she be grateful Graham was here, in her home and taking charge right here, right now, right when the man she'd loved for so long had finally returned? That odd thought she'd had about why Malcolm had chosen now to return niggled and she always listened to her instincts.

*At least . . . I'm learning to listen.*

If she'd done more listening and less rationalising of Malcolm's behaviour while they were together, would they still be together now?

*Or would I have left him long before he walked out on me?*

Her Catholic upbringing made that thought feel like

treachery. "Maybe we'll go with the kettle option, thanks, Graham."

He said nothing, but stood aside and held the door.

Malcolm stepped into her home, and Graham closed the door.

"I'll be in the kitchen if you need me."

"Thank you." She watched his retreating back and decided she was glad Graham was here. As for her ex-husband . . .

A maelstrom of conflicting emotions left her feeling light-headed. 'It's the same as grief,' Father Mulroney had counselled her. She'd experienced denial, anger, bargaining, depression, and finally acceptance.

But not forgiveness. She doubted she'd ever be able to forgive him.

"Sit down, Malcolm, and tell me what brings you back to town."

He sat on the couch where he used to sit back in their married home and raised an arm as though expecting her to take her usual spot. Nestling against him used to be wonderful and reassuring.

She sat in the armchair facing him and gripped the edges of her dressing gown together beneath her chin, conscious of her damp hair and lack of makeup. Malcolm had never liked seeing her less than neatly dressed.

His arm dropped and he jerked his head towards the

kitchen. "You and old Mugs, eh? What's that then?" The low light of the lamp gave his face a mean look. Mean and menacing.

"What do you—oh, it's not what you're thinking!"

"So he's not living with you?" Malcolm leaned back. Lamplight fell on his face and illuminated a sad smile.

Janice released her breath. Sad smile, not mean. Allowing her negative reaction to her ex-husband's sudden return wouldn't be helpful to a civilised, adult conversation.

"Not that it's any of your business, Malcolm. You gave up those rights when you left me, but we're—"

"Janice, do you want your camomile tea or a coffee?" Graham's question was neatly timed. So neat she wondered if he was cutting her off or saving her.

She had no idea how to describe their connection.

*Friends? Certainly.*

*Definitely more than acquaintances, but what—?* Until she'd worked it out she'd avoid that minefield. "Tea please."

"Decaf for me." Malcolm didn't bother looking at Graham. His attention focused on her and he smiled.

"We don't have decaf in this kitchen. Real coffee or tea, or water if you're not going to be here long." Graham's response took gruff to a whole new level of dislike.

Malcolm sneered. "Tea then. When are you leaving? I'd like to talk to my wife alone."

"Ex-wife, and I'll leave when Janice asks me to leave and

not a moment earlier."

An odd fluttery feeling tickled Janice's stomach, rose into her throat, settled in her chest. Testosterone bounced off the walls.

Graham's behaviour had morphed into active dislike, and Malcolm was clearly finding it difficult to juggle smiling at her and glaring at Graham.

Either she was hallucinating again, or deep in one of the strangest dreams she'd ever had.

Graham set the tray on the coffee table and handed a mug of tea to Janice. He picked up another mug, moved to the window next to Janice's and sipped his black coffee. *Let Bugalugs get his own drink.*

Most of what he knew about Malcolm Lehman came from Gei and her mother. Town gossip wasn't usually the most reliable source of information, but in this case, he reckoned the gossip mill had pegged the man accurately. Graham cracked open the window and stood in the breeze, observing the visitor.

Malcolm edged forward and reached for the last mug, half-rose before he could grasp the handle and cast a snide glance Graham's way. "Thanks for seeing me, Janice, although I—hoped to find you alone."

*And pining for you? Fat chance, chump.*

How Graham wished he could say that to Malcolm, but if there was any chance Janice wanted to get back with her ex,

Graham had no right to make it more difficult. Malcolm had made it clear he wished Graham gone.

What Janice thought was anyone's guess, but she hadn't asked him to leave her alone with her ex. That meant she wanted him, Graham, here.

For now.

Graham raised his mug and hid his grin with a gulp of coffee.

Janice wrapped both hands around her mug. "I don't know why you expected me to be alone, Malcolm. Just because you left me doesn't mean I'm unlovable."

Glad the mug hid any surprise in his expression, Graham narrowed his gaze on Janice.

Malcolm spluttered, the hand holding his tea jerked and tea splashed out.

"Hot. Damn." He raced into the kitchen and stuck his hand under cold water.

Graham watched without offering any help. Did Janice lack confidence? He would never have picked it judging by how she dealt with people, but he was the first to acknowledge he had no idea what women thought. Not these days. Then the implication of what she'd said hit him.

*She implied she's not unlovable because another man is in her house.*

*Me.*

How did he feel about being made complicit in her innocent deception? Was it a lie by omission if he said nothing?

He leaned back against the window and watched her more closely, the question he'd pushed to the back of his mind vying for his attention.

*Why did I choose to stay here and look after her? Rick said Gei or her mother would have come over, but I stopped him asking them. Why?*

She was a calm, practical woman, kind, attractive, caring. So caring that she'd tried to help him even as she was caught in the grip of the flu, or whatever bug had laid her low. The long and short of it was he liked her.

Malcolm returned to the lounge and carefully set the mug of tea on the table. He sat on the edge of the sofa and looked at Janice. "You're a wonderful woman. Honestly, I don't know why I ever left you. It was the wrong thing to do." He smiled in Janice's direction before his gaze crashed into Graham's. The smile slipped into a grimace that wished Graham to dissolve into nothing. "Look, Graham. This really isn't a conversation a bloke wants to have with an—onlooker. No offence, but could you give us some space."

Graham felt his grip tightening on the mug.

He looked at Janice. She was sitting very still. Behind her pale face and widening eyes, he had not a clue what she was thinking.

"Janice?" He looked directly at her. "Totally up to you."

## Chapter 8

"If you wouldn't mind giving us a few minutes please, Graham." Janice's smile was tight, but Graham's presence gave her strength and he was pleased to hear the resoluteness tinging her voice.

"I'll be outside." Graham gave nothing away, just nodded and took his mug of coffee with him. The front door closed quietly behind him.

Janice stared at the closed door and her heart thudded harder in her chest. For months after Malcolm deserted her she'd stared just so, willing, wanting, waiting for him to return and now he was here and she felt . . .

*What do I feel?*

The urge to jump up and call Graham back was strong. But that was just the lingering weakness of her illness talking. Illness and surprise. Stronger than both was pride in the knowledge she had made it through those dark days after Malcolm left her alone. She'd come out the other side.

She raised her head and met her ex-husband's gaze. "So you've come back to do what? Apologise for the *mistake* you made in leaving me, or for what you did that led to our last fight?"

"I did make a mistake." Malcolm set his mug on the coffee

table and came to sit in the armchair beside her. He reached for her hand.

Janice leaned away, resting an elbow on the side furthest from Malcolm. "What was your mistake? Leaving in the first place, or—

He frowned, a brief there-and-gone tightening of his forehead. The twin lines above his nose—lines she'd seen too often in the later years of their marriage—had deepened. Such lines, she now realised, were a sign of a discontented soul. Had she ever truly made him happy or had he always been a serially unhappy person?

"It's always been you for me, darling, and this time apart has made me see that we belong together. Give me a chance to make it up to you. I want to show you that we're still good together. We should be together."

"Together? As in the vows we made to care for each other in sickness and in health, till death do us part? I used to believe in my vows." Anger tinged her voice.

"What makes you think I want you back in my life?"

His expression shifted from pleading to something that seemed desperate.

"We could try again. Please, Janey?"

Oh God—his pet name for her pierced some tiny, almost-forgotten part of the love she'd once had for him. Her throat tightened around that nub of love, of memory. It choked her with sudden, overwhelming need.

*He left me. I didn't leave him. But . . . maybe we could . . .*

Graham's voice before he went outside sideswiped that treacherous need. *Totally up to you.*

*Up to me—my choice.*

Pushing to her feet—she needed every bit of control she had—she turned and looked down at Malcolm. "What makes you think I want anything to do with you now?"

He rose. Wisely he didn't try to approach her, but she couldn't look away from his blue gaze.

"I love you, Janey. Always have. I know I hurt you and I'm sorry. But please, let me begin to make it up to you."

"You can't just waltz back into my life as though the past year or so didn't happen. I've moved on—"

"With Graham, I get it. But you aren't sharing this house with him, are you? Where are his things? There's no sign of him in this room. Janey, tell me I'm not too late. Tell me you'll give me another chance with you. Please?"

"I want you to leave. Now."

A muscle jerked in Malcolm's jaw and his shoulders sagged. "My Janey would have offered another chance. But I'm not leaving town yet. I'm not going to give up without fighting for you, for us. I've taken a room at the hotel."

He walked to the door and stopped, his hand on the handle. He half turned and looked at her, sorrow in his eyes. "We were so good together. We could be good again."

Her head throbbed with anger and too much emotion as the door closed quietly behind him.

From the far corner of the dark garden, Graham watched Malcolm step onto the veranda and close the door. His stooped posture straightened, and, hands in pockets, he walked to his car as though he had not a care in the world.

Graham tossed the dregs of his coffee over the fence and watched the taillights of Lehman's car disappear over the rise in the road. He listened until the sound of the car sank into the night noises and was lost. He stood in the darkness until the soft lamplight in Janice's bedroom was switched off.

Only then did he quietly let himself into Janice's house. He collected the mugs from the coffee table, took them to the kitchen and washed them. Back in the hallway he looked at the closed door of Janice's bedroom. She was definitely on the mend—no more fever, no more spinouts; eating, albeit small amounts of food. She no longer needed anyone to keep an eye on her. He could return to the ridge with a clear conscience.

Except . . .

For the first time in thirty years, the thought of returning to his tent high on the hill didn't ease the constriction in his lungs that being around other people caused.

The thought of returning home felt—*lonely.*

But Janice had no more need of him.

Graham picked up his backpack, neatly stowed in the hallway cupboard and hoisted it onto one shoulder. Should he leave a note?

What would he say? *Don't trust your ex, he's a worm? I'll see you later for that dinner you offered?*

There was no point making a promise he wasn't sure he would keep. Or that Janice might not want to remember. Not now her former husband was back on the scene.

As quietly as he'd entered, Graham closed the front door behind him and slipped away into the night.

82

**Chapter 9**

"You're what?" The school secretary's voice rose in disbelief.

"I won't be in today and maybe not tomorrow. You'll need to get a relief teacher in to cover my class. There's work on my classroom desk so it should be an easy day." Janice couldn't remember the last time she'd had to take a sick day. Maybe when Malcolm left? She'd felt low then. Now she just felt weak and the thought of several high-energy hours with her class was beyond her.

"Let's lock in tomorrow as well, shall we? Bye, Rina." Janice ended the call. She wouldn't feel guilty about deserting her class; not when her leg muscles still trembled with the effort of standing.

Or was it because she'd walked out of her bedroom and found Graham had gone? Wrapping her dressing gown tightly around her, she held the lapels close beneath her chin and stepped onto the front veranda. Somewhere up on the ridge that dominated the western end of town, Graham was back in his eyrie. Was he happy to be home again?

*It's for the best.*

He hadn't come into town for Janice, the woman. She'd do well to remember that. He'd come seeking help from Janice

Lehman, the teacher. Graham was a compassionate man, but he struggled to be around people. Caring for her while she was ill must have used up his quota of people time for a month. *Maybe a year's worth.*

The westerly wind was blowing its last gasp. Janice shivered and hurried back inside. Today was perfect for a little pampering and relaxation. An exfoliating facemask, new nail polish on her toes, and a good book—her gaze fell on the John Grisham novel Graham had been reading, abandoned on the lamp table. A scrap of torn paper poked out of the closed novel, presumably marking the spot he'd reached yesterday.

She picked up the book. Whether she intended to pull the temporary bookmark out or just shelve the book she couldn't say, but a snippet of memory attached to the moments when they'd shared their mutual enjoyment of such stories.

Not for Malcolm. He scorned reading as being for those who didn't live in the real world before turning his attention to thugs cage-fighting on the television.

Something she loathed. The more she thought of it, the more she realised—they hadn't had much in common back then so why did he think they'd be good together now?

Something was off, but what?

With time to think and nothing to do but rest, she collected a fresh set of clothes and a new tub of face mud and headed into the main bathroom. Bubbles of foam and a good book might give her a fresh perspective.

The surveyor's peg worried Graham. He followed the almost invisible track skirting the Donovan farm to his winter campsite in the shell of a cottage behind the line of trees that dotted the lower slopes of the ridge. He turned and surveyed the wide view of Lark Creek and the town that shared its name. A wide view that might not remain his for much longer if this *intruder* was any indicator.

While he'd been looking after Janice, the marker and what it represented had slipped into the back of his mind. Not forgotten, but he'd had his work cut out managing his claustrophobia. Janice's time of need had helped.

*Was Rick right about it being therapeutic? Would I keep improving if I saw a specialist?*

Setting the thought aside now he was almost home, he stood looking at the nearest marker. The threat to his home hadn't disappeared.

Should he make an appointment to speak with Jack Donaldson? Would the lawyer be able to find out what applications were before council? More to the point, could he help Graham to stop whoever had sent the surveyors onto *his* mountain? Before he could second-guess himself, Graham stowed his backpack beneath a tree, turned and headed back down the hill.

As he approached the fifty-kilometre speed sign his boots

hit the first proper footpath. He passed the single storey building that marked the edge of the main part of town, and his lungs tightened.

What was it that had been different about staying at Janice's home? He'd managed to sleep on her couch for two nights—with occasional strolls around the garden. Was it the peace she exuded? Quiet surroundings and several paddocks between her home and the nearest neighbour were similar to the distance between his winter campsite and the Donovan farm.

Caring for her had forced him to deal with his claustrophobia in ways no one had required of him, ever. Was it possible he'd stumbled onto a way to become a real part of Rick's life?

A patch of shade lay beneath the awning over the front door of Jack Donaldson's office on the corner of the block—the quiet end of Main Street. Graham gritted his teeth and pushed open the front door.

Moira looked up from her computer and smiled. "Hello, Graham. Are you here to see Jack?"

"If he has time now, otherwise I'll make an appointment."

"I'll ask him. It's a quiet morning." She tapped on a door and entered.

Moments later, Jack followed Moira into the reception area and extended his hand. "Hello, Graham. Good to see you again. Come in." He led the way into his office and indicated a chair before settling into his own behind the oak desk. "How can I help?"

A heavy wooden bookcase took up most of one wall and a bank of three filing cabinets stood like soldiers along another. Light filtered through a set of Venetian blinds on one side and dust motes floated lazily in the stripes between the shadows.

Graham sucked in a breath and stared through the window behind Jack's head.

He blinked, focused on Jack's face, realised the lawyer was waiting for him to speak. "Can you find out who has put in surveyor's pegs up on the ridge?"

"I can find out recent applications for land rezoning. Is that what you mean?"

"I guess so. Look, someone's planted markers up on the ridge. A big area of land, maybe a similar size to the Donovan farm."

"Whoever it is, they haven't come to me for legal work." Jack tapped a pen on the desk and pulled a yellow legal notepad towards him. He wrote on the pad and then looked at Graham. "Does the area block your access to the ridge?"

"It may do. I couldn't find a corner marker to be sure."

"Do you own the land above the markers?"

Graham's heart sank. "Does it make any difference? I've lived up on that ridge for nigh on thirty years. It's my home."

"Are you saying you don't have any documents proving

ownership?"

"I don't."

"But you've lived up there for thirty years? Continuously?"

"Yes."

Jack frowned and began a search of some kind on his computer. "There are laws that might help if you can prove your continuous residence, but I'll need to check the requirements. Have you built any structures in the time you've been there?"

"I sleep in a tent when the weather's bad; outside, the rest of the time."

Jack added a few lines of writing on the pad.

Graham noticed two outsized question marks beside his last note. "There are a handful of people who know I live up there."

"Actually, I think most of Lark Creek knows you live there, but the key might be if anyone has actually seen you living up on the ridge."

"Rick has. He found me when he was about fourteen or fifteen. Stumbled across my campsite one day and kept coming back."

"Your son, Rick? So that must be, what—fifteen or so years ago?"

"At least that. More, I think."

"Leave it with me. I need to do some research. Do you have a phone number where—"

Graham held up a hand. "No phone. Never liked the things.

I'll come back into town. Just tell me when."

Jack clicked into the calendar on his computer. "I'm in court in Dalton doing a trial for the next couple of days. Look, if it's all the same to you, I'd like to see where you live, and you can show me the area where the markers are. How about you meet me next Saturday morning. Anna and I live in the cottage just near—" He gave a wry grimace. "You know where we live. Come down for breakfast and then we'll go take a look."

Graham stood and shook Jack's hand across the desk. "Thanks for that." He needed to get outside. He needed air. He needed . . . "I almost forgot. That copper friend of yours, the one who did the witness protection stuff."

"Smithy? What about him?"

"He's in charge of witness protection?"

"Not in charge, but he's got connections. Why?"

"I'm interested in doing more of it."

"I'll get in touch and let him know."

"Thanks. I'll see myself out." He turned on his heel. Only rigid self-discipline kept him from sprinting through the front door into the blessed open air. He dragged in a lungful of air and let his gaze slide up the street into the town proper. A silver city car, the same make and model as Malcolm Lehman had driven, turned out of the school gates and then took a road that led nowhere. Unless he counted a dead end as a destination and he doubted Lehman planned on going that far. Not when his ex-wife's house was on that road.

Graham stalked in the opposite direction towards the ridge and home.

The only difference between Janice's home and every other building he'd been in was—Janice. Was she the reason he'd found the strength to stay inside?

Soft notes of classical music faded as Janice emerged from her bubble bath. Her skin felt soft after the mud mask, and a long soak in hot bubbles had restored her energy level. The rest of the day stretched ahead.

She raised her arms and stretched, feeling deliciously lazy. Her fluffy bathrobe—an indulgence on her last trip into Toowoomba—slipped over skin sensitised by pampering. With a tug and a flick, she loosened her hair from the headband and finger-combed it. Stepping into her sheepskin slippers, she wriggled her toes in the soft lining and then dabbed moisturiser onto her forehead and cheeks.

Satisfied and relaxed, Janice hummed as she strolled into the kitchen and made a cup of herbal tea. As good as she was feeling, her stomach was still—*delicate*. Operating on autopilot, she opened the fridge and reached for a carton of milk at the same time as she remembered she'd made a herbal brew.

An unfamiliar pottery jug covered with plastic wrap sat on the nearly empty top shelf. She lifted it out, eased up one side of the covering and took a tentative sniff. Just able to make out a hint of something lemony, it struck her.

*This is the last of the soup Graham made for me.*

She blinked away silly tears that threatened to fall and sniffed. Why on earth was she turning on the waterworks over soup, for goodness sake!

It wasn't as though nobody else had made a meal for her, although Malcolm had never . . .

No, she wasn't going down that road. Comparing two men with very different personalities was unworthy of her. They simply had different skill sets and different priorities.

But it had been nice, being looked after for once in her life.

Setting the pottery jug on the bench, she smoothed the plastic cover firmly around the rim. It would make a welcome dinner this evening. As she set the jug back in the fridge three loud knocks rapped on the front door.

Elated that Graham hadn't simply left without a word, but curious why he was knocking, she scurried to the door and stopped, hand on the knob, self-conscious about wearing little more than a bathrobe.

*For goodness sake, he's seen me in my PJs.*

Pinning a smile on her face she opened the door.

"Hello, darling." Malcolm leaned in and kissed her.

At the last second, she turned her head, so he connected with her cheek. "Malcolm, what are you doing here?"

A flash of something that might have been displeasure at being thwarted darted through his eyes. "I told you last night. I want to get back with you. When the woman in your school office told me you weren't coming into work today, I knew you must have been really sick. You never took time off before. Though I must say I expected you'd be dressed by . . ." He flicked a glance at his watch.

The flashy, chunky gold watch was new. It looked expensive and probably was. Malcolm had never liked anything less than the best.

"Hmm, it's half-past ten. But of course, you've been ill. Any chance of a cuppa?"

"*Really*, Malcolm?" Sharp edges in her voice were rare, moments confined to difficult students going beyond what was acceptable. Sharp edges were for pulling a child back from a dangerous situation. And for ex-husbands asking for cuppas when she was barely back on her feet.

The women in Malcolm's family had always done everything for him, and she'd fallen into the habit when they married.

He seemed taken aback, only for a moment, but then he rallied. "Let me make one for you. I came to talk, to convince you that I mean what I said. I really want us to make a fresh start. Can I come in and do that, Janey?"

In the first few days after he'd walked out, she'd have

given anything for him to appear at her door, telling her he'd made a mistake, wanting to return to her.

Now, he was behaving like some whiny, whinging, spoilt brat.

There was no flutter in her stomach, no little kick of a thrill like her young heart had felt when smooth city boy, Malcolm Lehman started showing interest in her.

There was no need to be held by him, crushed to his chest and told she was the only woman for him.

Those feelings had evaporated like rain off hot bitumen.

"Things have changed. I've changed. I've moved on since I wasn't the one who left." But a small kernel of memory of what they'd shared lingered, a spark that had never quite been extinguished despite the gaping hole his departure had ripped in her psyche. It made her body step back and open the door, admitting him into her loungeroom. "Oh, come in out of the cold."

She'd no sooner let him in than she regretted not shutting the door in his face.

"You're doing the right thing, Janey. This will be so good."

She shut the door behind him and headed into the kitchen. "I still don't have decaf." Refilling the electric kettle from the tap, she couldn't decide how Malcolm's surprise return made her feel.

Nervous?

A little.

Angry?

A lot.

But beneath the nerves and the anger and the surprise and the uncertainty lurked something more. She felt emotionally stronger than she'd felt in all the years of their marriage and her sense of self-worth and identity were . . .

Water sloshed over the rim of the kettle and down the front of her bathrobe. She jumped back and looked down. A puddle of water was forming around her slippers.

"Bother."

A small snort escaped.

Until she had a better handle on exactly why Malcolm had chosen this moment to come back into her life she'd treat him politely, but with caution.

There was no way she'd allow him to break her heart all over again, but something was definitely off about his visit.

## Chapter 10

Graham banked the campfire and emptied the dregs of his coffee. Breakfast called, courtesy of Jack at Cottage Farm, but it wouldn't do to arrive too early. Graham was well aware that today was the weekend. Jack worked hard all week and time off with loved ones was precious. And while Kaden might have brought Jack and Anna together, they were now definitely an item, albeit a relatively new item as relationships went.

He looked around for Jacqueline. Sounds of her scratching for grubs in dry leaves told him she was foraging for her breakfast. For the second day in a row there'd been no egg laid in his old beanie, which Jacky had appropriated for her nest.

"See you later, Jacky. Don't disturb any sleeping snakes while I'm gone."

Silence from Jacqueline.

Graham sighed. The taste of companionship with Janice had been all too brief. Too brief and at the same time, too long. He missed the little interactions that had marked his days in her house. He missed discovering shared tastes and interests. And he missed doing little things to help her as she lay sick in bed.

And now the jerk was back in town. Graham had seen his car cruising the main street earlier in the day.

Doubt reared its head as Graham thought about the hours he'd spent with Janice.

*Why would she want* me *in her life?*

Feeling both annoyed and despondent at the poor timing of Lehman's reappearance, Graham shrugged into a sleeveless puffy vest and set off down the hill. He wouldn't look at the marker poles. He wouldn't let their malign presence on his ridge affect his earlier good mood, or the promise of a hot breakfast.

*White against green, white against stone.*

The white markers snagged his attention as he strode along the barely visible path. Glaring at the nearest pole did nothing more than raise his blood pressure.

He shoved his hands into the pockets of his cargo pants and set his sights on Dawnie Farm and beyond that, a magnificent stand of trees, surely planted when the first settlers took up their selection. Two aged oak trees and assorted smaller trees sheltered Cottage Farm from the worst of the westerly winds.

By the time he reached the fence line between the farms, a regular *chop-chop-crack* replaced his fixation on the offensive markers, and when he closed the gate and turned towards the shed, he saw Jack wielding an axe and stacking firewood beneath the lean-to roof.

He took a deep breath before he stopped outside the woodchip splattered dirt circle surrounding the chopping block. "Morning." Graham waited for Jack to bed the axe into the wood block and then extended his hand.

Jack swiped his right hand over the seat of his work trousers and then shook hands. "Good to see you're early. Anna's keen to catch up with you. Have you heard from Kaden recently?"

"No phone, no computer, so, no."

"Then I'm sure she'll be happy to update you. He sent photos and an email. Come on around to the kitchen."

Graham followed Jack up the back steps, unlaced and toed off his boots and stood them beside a full shoe rack. He could manage a meal inside. He'd had more meals inside a house in the past week than in the past year.

His stomach muscles tightened, but not in that *I'm about to throw up* way that had kept him living on the ridge. Was it because he felt in control of where he went, of what he did?

Anna Wilkins appeared in the doorway holding a laden tray of eggs, bacon and sausages in her hands. Her smile was genuine and open, much more relaxed than when he'd first met her months ago. Back then, they'd worked together to connect with a deaf teenager and then whisked him away in the dead of night barely minutes ahead of his underworld uncle.

"Lovely to see you, Graham."

"Thanks for the offer of breakfast."

"Our pleasure. I thought we'd eat out here and enjoy the view." She moved past him.

Graham turned. A simply set table for three filled one end

of the fly-screened veranda.

Anna rested the tray on one corner of the small table and set a colourful plate of food at each setting.

Jack reappeared from the kitchen with a second, smaller tray holding a plate piled high with toast and a pot of tea. He set the tray on top of the wood box within easy reach of his hand. "I like eating out here when the weather's reasonable. Hope you don't mind."

"I prefer it too, thanks."

Jack gestured for Graham to sit and held a chair for Anna before taking his own. "I think I have some idea of how you feel about being inside after my own brief incarceration. It's been months and still there are moments when I find myself having what I think is a mild panic attack. Tell me, does it ever get any easier?"

"You were locked up? What for?" He couldn't imagine the lawyer doing anything wrong, much less being in jail for any crime. "Don't they disbar you for that?"

Anna spluttered and laughed out loud. "Darling, I think Graham thinks you were in jail."

"Jail—what, no! Hickman's thugs tossed me through the trapdoor in our kitchen and bolted it. I was trussed up like a roast chook for Sunday lunch with an egg-sized lump on the back of my head for good measure. No idea how long I was in there, but I thought I'd die before anyone found me." His lips snapped shut and the muscles in his cheeks rippled with an effort Graham recognised.

He knew how hard it was to hold back a scream, a whimper, a plea to be released. Beneath the shelter of the yellow tablecloth, he clenched his hands. "It's not a good feeling."

Anna touched his arm lightly. "Tell me to butt out if I'm out of line, but I know you have a problem with claustrophobia. Were you trapped somewhere that caused it, or . . ." She trailed off, the question incomplete, but understood.

"Sort of. My problem developed after—an incident. If you want a positive answer, I'm the wrong man to ask. I've lived up there on O'Reilly's Ridge nigh on thirty years because it hasn't."

Jack's face tightened. The same bleakness flitted through his eyes as Graham had seen in his own.

"But that's me and my situation. Doesn't mean the memories won't fade in time for you."

Anna bit her bottom lip. "I'm sorry, I didn't mean to raise unpleasant memories." She reached for Jack's hand, clenched like Graham's, only his rested beside his plate, and covered it with hers. "We can always move back into town, Jack. We don't have to stay here."

Jack took a slow, audible breath and let it out in a quick huff of air. "I won't let it beat me. There must be ways of dealing with the psychological effects. I just need to find what works for me."

"Maybe a therapist?"

"Did you see anyone, Graham?" Anna's tone was light, not pushing for an answer if he didn't have one to give, but keen, wanting to know, wanting anything that could help Jack. It was clear how much she loved him in the way her gaze lighted on him and her lips tipped up when he looked at her.

Graham sprinkled salt and pepper over his fried eggs and cut into the soft yolk. It oozed and spread around the sausages.

*Like blood from a head wound.*

*Stop thinking that way. This isn't a war zone.*

He dropped the knife and fork on his plate and met Anna's eyes. "No. Maybe it would have helped. I don't know. What I do know is that it's better to try and do something than live with that sort of shit unresolved. Demons have to be confronted to be defeated."

He half-expected to hear a roll of thunder or a brassy fanfare following his announcement. Something to mark the moment of his epiphany, thirty years later.

What he got was: "I think you're right, don't you agree, Jack?"

Jack sighed and gave a wry grin. "Anna's been on at me to talk to someone about my *traumatic ordeal* since she and Kaden came back. I kind of hoped you'd be on my side."

Graham rested his elbows on the table and leaned forward. "Son, I am on your side. Go talk to someone. If you love this woman, go and get your head sorted out so you can move on with your lives together."

Jack nodded. "I will. Next week."

"First thing Monday morning, my love?" Anna squeezed his hand.

Their gazes connected, locking them in a mini-bubble where nothing existed but each other.

Graham picked up his cutlery and concentrated on enjoying a hot meal he hadn't prepared on his campfire. He was happy for Jack and Anna, so why did seeing the love they shared make him feel empty? He'd known his one true love. A man couldn't ask for more than that in one lifetime.

"Tea, Graham?"

He looked up. Jack held the teapot over a mug, one eyebrow raised.

"Yes. Thanks." Light conversation followed, but Graham's mind dipped in and out. One person occupied his thoughts.

Maybe he'd call in and check on Janice tomorrow—just to make sure she had fully recovered. He could say he'd dropped by to pick up his jug.

And see if Lehman was still sniffing around and if he wasn't . . .

What could Graham offer any woman?

## Chapter 11

Graham stopped beside the second-to-last marker and pointed out the location of the last one. "See what I mean?"

Jack lightly kicked the marker with his boot and looked around the area they'd walked. "It's a substantial parcel of land all right. Big enough to have a major impact on those of us living out this side of town—big enough to affect the economy of Lark Creek too, I expect."

Graham's insides twisted, threatening to expel his breakfast in short order. "I was off on the far side of the creek for a couple of days. I didn't see the surveyors, or I'd have asked what the hell they were doing."

"I doubt they'd have revealed any details. Speaking of which, so far all I've managed to find is a company name and a receiving office for mail in Brisbane. Does the name, Fiesta Holdings, mean anything to you?"

"No. Can you track down the owner and find out what they want with a parcel of land so far from the city?"

"I've asked a friend in Brisbane to look into it for me." He turned his back on the marker and looked at the view. "Wow. Last time I was up here we were running for our lives. I didn't stop to appreciate the view, but I can see the attraction of living up here. It has the three things most people look for in their home—location,

location, location."

"And peace and quiet. Everyone's at a distance and I aim to keep it that way, with your help." It wasn't greed driving Graham. Owning land had never been a priority, not even back when he'd married Alice. But without the safety barrier that plenty of distance from people offered, he'd lose more than the sanctuary that was his home. Isolation had helped him retain his sanity.

Glancing through the trees at the towering upper peaks of the ridge, calm settled over him. In the early years, when his PTSD had been all consuming and so much worse, before he'd worked out a handful of coping mechanisms, he'd made plans and bought rope.

There was always a way out.

Jack had pulled his phone from his pocket and was slowly panning across the space. "Got it. Now, where's your campsite?"

"Not far. I'll show you."

Graham led the way through the trees, stopping beside the banked fire. "Might not be much in most people's eyes, but it's home."

Jacqueline came running, her short chicken legs giving her a rolling sailor's gait as she made a beeline for Graham.

He scooped her up, settled her into the crook of his arm, and petted her. "Complete with resident pet. Say hello to Jack, Jacky."

Jack reached out and gently scratched the chicken's head,

but his gaze was fixed on the ruins. "Did you build the fireplace?"

"You call that pile of stones a fireplace? No, I just added a few more to what was left of the old cottage. Maybe the second winter I was here. That was a bad winter in more ways than one."

"Talk me through it. You lived in what was left of the cottage twenty- or thirty-something years ago?"

"Yep. Patches of roof still existed back then, attached to a chimney and that far corner. There was even a doorframe. I used the wood to start a fire." He jerked his thumb at the low stone wall protecting his campfire. "That winter was the worst I've lived through—here. Winds like you wouldn't believe, and snow fell— can you believe it?"

"So you sheltered in the cottage."

"Better than being caught in the open, but it was a ruin even then. That winter finished it off. The roof over the chimney caved in and most of the chimney blew down. I built enough of the old fireplace up to protect my campfire, but it was damned cold. In the end, I retreated into a cave higher up."

"But you lived here that second winter? And now. What about the intervening years? Do you live here year-round?"

Graham considered Jack a measured man; little seemed to disturb his equanimity, but there was a sharp edge of interest in his voice. "Not year-round, no. It's more like a base camp."

"As in, home?"

"If home means returning to the one spot then yes, I guess

so."

"Did you leave any gear, any possessions here? Anything that might mark this spot as your home?"

"Sure. Even living rough like I do, there are a handful of tools I don't take with me when I move camp during the summer. Higher up you can catch a breeze. Most nights up there I sleep under the stars."

"Good, good." Jack made no notes, but his tone sharpened. "Did Rick visit you here, in this exact location all those years ago? At other times?"

Interest morphed into the closest Graham had heard Jack get to being excited.

He was banging on about home so much, it must be important.

Graham looked around the campsite and dredged for a memory. A tall teenager, all awkward angles and gangling limbs, had emerged from the old path, his expression angry and hurt. *How old was Rick when I saw him then—fourteen or fifteen?*

Something about the troubled teenager had changed Graham's usual response to intruders on his patch of the mountain. He'd still been offhand—taciturn, Alice would have called him— but he'd let Rick stay and shown him a thing or two about tracking.

"The first time he climbed the ridge, he stumbled into my camp. This place. Came back most weekends after that. He never said much for months on end." They'd forged a friendship during those visits.

"How old is Rick now? About thirty?" Jack pulled out his phone and took a number of photos, the soft clicking barely discernible as he captured different angles of the ruins and Graham's camp.

"Thirty-two last birthday."

"I'll need to talk to Rick and find out what he remembers, but you may have a case to make under adverse possession—"

"English please."

"Squatter's rights, sort of. I'll research further and contact an old uni friend who specialises in property law."

"So you think I have a chance against this developer?" It had been a long shot asking for Jack's help, but worth the stress of visiting him in town if he could stay on his mountain.

"I don't want to raise your hopes at this stage, but I believe we have a reasonable chance."

Graham nodded, but Jack's *at this stage* worried him. He rubbed his thumb over his bottom lip.

He took a deep breath. It had to be said, and now rather than later. "I appreciate what you've done for me, but I can't afford a long drawn-out case. I'm sorry. I should have made that clear from the beginning. I will pay you for the work you've done, but—"

"Not a problem, Graham. I understand. Most people prefer to avoid litigation as far as possible, but consider this. Anna and I live down the hill. Whichever way you look at it, we, and probably the Donovan family, are likely to be affected by any development or rezoning application here."

"Jack, I'm not looking for charity—" His gut churned at the mere idea of it. Just because he chose to live the way he did, didn't mean he had nothing. One glance around his campsite could never reveal how lucky he considered himself.

"I'm not offering any. What I propose is that, as soon as I have more information, we get together with the Donovans and talk; hopefully sometime next week. I'll call into the farmhouse on the way home and let them know as much as we do and find out if they're interested in joining with us."

He slipped the phone into his shirt pocket and spread his hands. Turning in a slow circle, his wide arms encompassed Graham's campsite and the ridge beyond before taking in the surveyed land below. "This affects each of us, Graham. It's not your burden to bear alone. We'll share the costs."

"Fine. How much do you need me to put into your trust account?" *Can I afford even a third of a court case—if it reaches that stage?*

"I'll let you know once I have an idea what, or who, we're dealing with. Deal?" He held out his hand.

Graham shook hands. There had to be a way to make this work. "Deal. Thanks."

Jack rubbed his hands together. "Nothing I like better than

diving into a new David-and-Goliath case. Of course, it may be a single businessman and not some faceless corporation we're up against, but I enjoy a challenge. I'll let you know as soon as I've heard back from my mate in Brisbane."

Jack sauntered down the track whistling a tune, something modern Graham didn't recognise.

Smoke curled up from the fireplace and Graham assessed his woodpile. Enough for the day, but clear skies meant night-time temperatures would dive and a frost was likely. He picked up the canvas sheet he used to keep his supply of wood dry and set off into the trees, Jacky trailing behind.

Who would have thought building up a fireplace and leaving a few tools under cover made this a home?

He stopped abruptly in the middle of a small clearing.

Janice's place felt a bit like home with Alice used to feel. Was that why he'd managed to stay inside for so long?

Jacky ran into his booted foot and squawked a disgusted protest.

Distracted, he glanced down at the chicken, his lone companion since Kaden had left. "Sorry, old girl." But his thoughts circled around the idea, coming back to a single, immutable fact. Home had been wherever Alice was.

Was it a person who made a place a home?

He was no closer to an answer by the time he returned to camp, a load of fallen wood for his fire slung over his shoulder.

By the time Janice reached the marker pole near the line of trees, pointed out to her by Anna Wilkins, she was hot, bothered, and out of breath.

The wind had dropped to an occasional light puff, but the day was still on the cool side, and yet she was a sweating, legs-trembling mess. Tendrils of loose hair stuck to her forehead and cheeks. Her hand rose to push them back where they belonged, but what was the point? She was destined to look less than her best whenever she met Graham. If she could find him.

Shrugging her daypack into a more comfortable position on her shoulders, she blew out an audible breath.

Telling herself off seldom worked, but she tucked one more sticky strand of hair behind her ear and trudged on towards where she hoped to find Graham's campsite.

Breathing harder than such a climb would usually make her, she stopped and lifted her head. Woodsmoke scented the breeze. Which direction did it come from?

Since last week's illness, the ability to smell anything properly still surprised her, but it meant she must be close to his camp. Cupping her mouth, she sent out a "Coo-eee," long and loud like her father had taught her; he'd be proud of the sound she produced.

Through the trees ahead she made out movement and, a moment later, Graham appeared.

"Janice? What are you doing here?" He stopped a few metres from her, too far for her to read the expression in his eyes.

Was he pleased to see her? Annoyed that she was disturbing him? At the best of times he was a hard man to read. With sweat blurring her vision, it was impossible.

Standing as straight as the slope of the path and her tired body would allow, she mentally gritted her teeth. What did she have to lose?

I'm here now, she reminded herself, and smiled. "Hi. I come bearing gifts. And to return your jug." Why couldn't she *not* be puffing like a steam train? Or falling in a heap at his feet. It seemed she was destined never to meet him when she was looking her best?

She stretched her smile wider.

"You know how to send out a fine *coo-eee*." His compliment made her feel better. He made her feel good about herself.

"My father taught me. I imagine you do can do it too."

"I have more reason to imitate birds. Do it well and it's hard to tell from the real thing."

"What's your favourite?"

"Depends. The Mopoke is handy." He cupped his hands and sent out an *oom, oom* sound.

"I'm impressed. I bet most people wouldn't know that wasn't the owl calling."

He held out one hand. "Let me take your backpack for you."

"It's fine, thanks. It's not far to your camp, is it?" She prayed it wasn't or it might be the third time she collapsed, and he came to her rescue.

"No, not far." Graham waited for her to reach him before he turned and strolled ahead, leading the way. He stepped to one side and a small clearing opened up before her eyes. "This is it."

His voice suddenly turned gruff; the three words clipped. He folded his arms and simply stood there. Except there was nothing casual about his stance. The air around him vibrated with tension.

She wondered why he was defensive, worse than the night they'd had a drink in the pub. He wasn't even inside.

Was he embarrassed about his home, or that she was seeing it?

She eased the daypack off her shoulders and lowered it, looking around. "You're so lucky to live here, Graham. It's beautiful."

And it was.

Janice breathed deeply, smelling the air and soaking in what was a truly lovely place.

Winter sunlight picked out blue-grey tints in the upper branches of the eucalyptus trees and filtered softly onto lower bushes. Around her, Graham's campsite had the appearance of having been raked clear. Small branches were stacked in a neat pile next to a campfire, built into what might once have been a cottage fireplace. In the corner opposite the fireplace a canvas tent hung over a pole wedged into the forks of a pair of low-branching trees. The front flaps were tied back with plaited strips of natural fibre. The contents were folded or stowed in open-fronted wooden cubes.

A soft sigh caught her attention.

If he was uncomfortable with her seeing where he lived, she'd have to show him differently. "You couldn't have chosen better than here. It's the best spot on the ridge and you've made it yours. The scent of those flowering native plants is divine. They must love it up here. There are so many more than I've seen closer to town."

"I planted them for my bees."

"I didn't know you had beehives." She thought of the jar of local honey in her pantry, the hand-drawn label—the name! Could it be a coincidence? Watching for his reaction she asked, "Are you responsible for Wild Ridge Honey?"

He evaded her gaze and tossed another log onto the fire, stirring the coals.

"You are!"

He gave her an embarrassed glance. "What gave me away?"

"The name. And seeing all these flowering trees together and smelling the scent—it's just like—I guess it *is* the honey I buy at the markets."

"Nobody knows about it except Rick, and now Gei and her family. I'd prefer if it stays that way. Too many people tramping through the area will unsettle the bees."

"I won't say a word. I don't betray my friends, Graham, but I'm delighted. I've enjoyed Wild Ridge honey for years. To think this is where it originates." She plucked a leaf from a grevillea growing next to the ruined cottage and ran it between her fingers. "You can't buy any more local than this. Do you mind if I sit near the fire?"

"I'll get you a chair. Hang on." He brought out a camping chair and set it near the fire, banged the seat with one hand and stood back. "This is more comfy than sitting on a log."

"Thanks." Gratefully she sank into the faded canvas seat and leaned back. She stretched her legs towards the warmth of the fire. "So, did you plant all those flowering bushes for your bees?"

"Most of them. There were only a few when I first started living up here, but once I noticed which ones the bees preferred, I planted more. As the bee population increased, I divided the hives and added other compatible and complementary plants." Graham lifted the lid off a black billycan, peered into it and then finally met her gaze. "Cuppa?"

"Please and thank you."

He hung the billy over the flames and set two enamel mugs on a flat stone near the fire.

She could have watched him all day.

It wouldn't do to let him see that, but the more she came to know Graham, the more fascinating she found him. There was so much more to him than what the town knew, or made up about the hermit on the hill.

Graham was complex and kind, a beekeeper, a protector . . .

Janice gazed into the flames. Hypnotic, flickering, dancing . . . it was comforting, reminding her of happier times.

How often she had sat on the ground beside Danny and Dad, with Mum in a camping chair. They were less complicated times, carefree times, times before her parents sold off the farm after her brother died.

Before she found and lost love.

She blinked away the tears that were never far when she thought of Danny, even two years on. It was meant to get easier with time.

"You're far away." She blinked and realised Graham had drawn up a canvas stool beside her. "Where were you, Janice?"

"In the past." Where her brother was still alive, but she wasn't ready to share that with Graham. Not yet.

"I love watching open flames, especially at night. When I was a girl, my father used to take us out camping pretty often. I loved it, but my mother had a bad back and—

"Sorry, I'm babbling."

Not that Graham seemed to be put off by her flood of

personal memories.

He was a gentleman, and he was kind. Firsthand experience of his kindness had created this friendship between them. But she couldn't bring herself to tell him about Danny. Not yet. Not until she got her emotions under control.

"Well, that's what I was thinking about. I miss those days."

"Sounds like a great childhood. Did you grow up in Lark Creek?" He lifted the lid of the billy. Apparently satisfied with what he saw, he set the billy beside the mugs and added a handful of tea leaves.

"Yes. Our farm was out near Freda Moloney's property. Her family and mine were two of the earliest selections to be taken up in this district."

"Is your family still there?"

That wretched lump of loss and sorrow rose, blocking her throat, stopping her words. She coughed, attempting to dislodge it and find her voice.

"Is the smoke getting to you? Let me move your chair."

Shaking her head and raising a hand, she created a few precious seconds to get her emotions under control. "No, I'm fine, thanks. How do you make your billy tea?"

A narrow-eyed, piercing gaze watched her for several heartbeats before he reached for the billy. "Like this." He picked it up and swung the open billy half a dozen times in an arc and then set it near the fire to brew.

"My father was an old bushie and he made it the same way, but with the addition of a carefully chosen eucalyptus leaf."

"One not chewed by a koala?"

Janice laughed. "That's right. He used to get Danny and I to hunt for the perfect leaf. It couldn't have bite marks or black spots, and boy, did we compete to be the one to find that leaf."

"That's a good memory to hold onto." He poured tea into the mugs and handed one to her. "There's honey if you want it sweetened."

She smiled and shook her head, making more of smelling the tea than it warranted, mostly so she didn't have to meet Graham's perceptive gaze. What was it about him that she mentioned Danny when she'd decided not to?

"I'll give you your jug and that little extra I mentioned. I'd hate to forget either." She placed the mug under her chair and set her daypack on her lap to unzip it. "Here's your jug, with many thanks for the contents. And I baked some Anzac biscuits."

"You didn't need to, but thanks." He took the jug and sat it next to the fire.

"And that dinner invitation—I haven't forgotten. Does next Saturday about six o'clock suit?"

"I'll be there. Although—" He frowned, but left the sentence hanging.

"What's the problem? You aren't going to back out because you don't like walking in the dark, are you?" Her smile trembled around the edges, as insecure as she felt negotiating this unexpected friendship with a man most people called a hermit.

"Will anyone else be there?"

Tone—neutral; body language—apparently relaxed.

But his shoulders were as stiff as a wooden coat hanger.

The mug rose to his lips.

She couldn't pick any other change in his tone or body language, unless she counted that watchfulness he shared with his son. Beneath the simple question lay a world of possibilities, but which was this? Graham's instant dislike of Malcolm; or did it have more to do with his dislike of crowds?

"If I say it's just the two of us will I send you running for the hills?"

"Why would I do that? I like your company."

"You do?"

"You're easy to talk to." His gaze slid away. He turned and added another piece of wood to the fire.

Maybe it was no more than close proximity to the heat, but Janice could have sworn he'd blushed before he turned to the fire.

"It helps that we share some common interests. By the way, I brought that novel you were reading with me. You're welcome to borrow it if you want to finish. I left your bookmark in place."

Graham poked at the perfectly good fire, sending sparks into the air. "That'd be good, thanks. Are you up to walking just a little further? There's a grand place to look out from."

"I'd like that." She swallowed the last of her tea and looked around for where to put the mug.

"I'll take that. It's not far but bring water if you have a bottle. You're not long out of your sick bed."

Having handed over the novel, Janice pulled an almost full bottle of water from her pack, looked at it and picked up the slim daypack. "Might as well carry it in this and keep my hands free."

With nothing more than a nod, Graham set off uphill, his pace sedate and his conversation, nil.

Silence with Graham was comfortable. Comfortable and comforting. And Janice let her thoughts wander, soaking in the simple pleasure.

Birds twittered at their passing as they climbed steadily. As slow as Graham took it, Janice had to stop for a breather and a drink.

"I thought you said it wasn't far?"

"We're nearly there."

"Your idea of *nearly there* and mine are a little different, I think."

He grinned, the smile dropping several years from his face. "It's just around this bend. I promise."

"Fine. Just around this bend. Lead on, Macduff." She capped the water bottle and shoved it back in the stretchy side pocket of her pack. Gulping an extra deep breath, she plodded on, one foot in front of the other following Graham.

Literally ten metres around the bend, he stopped beside a massive boulder. "Told you. Man of my word."

Janice leaned against the cool stone, speechless. They were two-thirds of the way to the beginning of the saddle-shaped top of the hill. Above them the track petered out and the ridge rose, dark and forbidding from this angle. Below, flashes of sunlight shimmered on the creek, and the sloping hill that led up to Thornyhill Farm on the far side of the valley. And in the middle Lark Creek lay indolently soaking up the winter sunshine.

"The air is so clear I feel like I can see forever."

"That clarity means we'll have a frost tonight. You might want to throw a cover over that lemon tree of yours."

"You noticed the lemon tree? Of course you did. Do you know a lot about plants?"

"Mostly natives. I experimented with various plants over the years. At first it was mainly those I grew for the bees, and then it expanded when I began making gin. Rick bases the products he sells in The Gin Joint on my recipes and I supply the botanicals."

Pride rang in his voice and Janice felt a pang of envy, like a sharp wedge of pain in the region of her heart.

How she had longed to have a child of her own, one whose joys and sorrows she could share in. A child to talk about with her friends with those casual references others dropped into conversation. Did they realise how lucky they were? Did they appreciate what it meant to hold that special place in a child's heart?

"Janice, are you okay?"

Graham's question and a gentle touch on her shoulder brought her back to the present. Surprised to find her vision blurred by tears, she pulled a tissue from her pocket and blew her nose defiantly. "Perfectly fine, thank you. Just a touch of hay fever. Thanks for bringing me up here and showing me the view, but I really think I need to head home."

"I'll walk you back."

"There's no need. My car is parked near Anna Wilkins' cottage."

"Fine, I'll walk you to your car and if you like, I'll come with you and help to cover your plants. Protecting them from frost is important. Besides, if I ask nicely, would you give me a couple of lemons from that bush of yours?"

The request was simple, one a neighbour or friend might ask. That the request had come from Graham and that he was comfortable enough with *her* to even ask it meant a lot.

"Take as many as you want. It's a steady producer, that one."

On their way back to her ute, Graham popped into his tent and retrieved a bottle of his homemade gin, banked the fire and closed the flaps of his tent.

By the time they reached the flat stretch where she'd parked her ute, Janice was grateful for Graham's helping hand across the ditch. She gripped his hand tightly. Maybe she held on for longer than she needed to, but her leg muscles trembled as much as they had thirty years earlier when she'd climbed all the way to the top of O'Reilly's Ridge with Danny. She remembered the trembling; she hadn't liked it then either, but the view from the top had been great compensation.

This time all she'd done was a short hike up a slope. How could she have overestimated her capability so badly so soon after being sick?

"Since I'm coming with you, would you like me to drive?" Graham's offer out of the blue was a godsend. Surprising, but very welcome. Had he felt her tremors when she took his hand?

Her legs were so wobbly she'd probably stall the damned car and that would be mortifying.

"I'm happy, if you don't mind driving."

Graham opened the passenger door and waited while she removed her pack and settled into the seat before he climbed in behind the wheel.

They drove home in companionable silence until they crested the rise in the road leading to Janet's driveway. Parked under her carport was a silver sedan.

Janice leaned forward and gripped the dashboard. "Damn it, what's he doing here again?"

Blasted Lehman again. Graham's inner warrior growled.

The adrenaline surge hit hard. Hands tight on the steering wheel, he peered through the windscreen, muscles at action stations. Was his reaction no more than the fact Janice's ex-husband had hurt such a decent woman, or was it that Lehman was a slimy bastard through and through and Graham didn't want Janice anywhere near the man?

"Do you still want me to come in and cover the tree for you, or would you prefer I leave now?" He glanced across at her.

Janice was frowning and one hand plucked at the material of her hiking trousers. "Please don't go. I offered you coffee and cake and I don't like going back on my word."

Taking his lead from Janice, he worked hard to respond in a civil manner. "Cake? Homemade too, I presume?" And the invitation pleased him. It pleased him because it signalled that Lehman—the worm—hadn't managed to insinuate himself back into Janice's good graces. *Yet.* But in the back of his mind, tucked away where he couldn't examine its meaning too closely, her offer also made him feel good—good, or wanted?

"Yes. I enjoy baking. It's been a while since I had anyone other than my colleagues to bake for." Her cheeks pinked up. "Oh, don't take that the wrong way."

"There is no wrong way when you've done something kind, but in that case I'm even more honoured by your gift." Graham turned the ute into the driveway and pulled up on the far side of the carport. Glancing through the driver's side window at Janice's ex-husband, he did a mental chest thump.

Janice baked for me, so shove that in your pipe and smoke it, he thought.

He went around the front of the car and opened Janice's door. The ground was dry and there were bare patches of dirt, but Lehman had usurped her spot under the carport and Graham wanted nothing—not even coming back outside to move the ute—to delay Lehman's departure. Even better if that happened within the next thirty seconds, but he wouldn't hold his breath.

"I'll put your pack inside and then go around the back and find something to cover the lemon tree."

"Thank you. There should be a pile of hessian bags in the shed next to the mower." Janice handed her small pack to him with a quick smile of thanks that was gone before she looked over at her ex-husband.

It seemed she hesitated a moment and pulled her shoulders back before slipping on a different smile, as though she was putting on makeup. This smile, social, small, and lukewarm, reassured Graham.

Until he saw her eyes.

Was there a spark deep within—a spark of anger? Or of hope? If the latter, it undercut his hopes like a landslip, and the brief flash of pleasure when she'd asked him to stay sidled away, hanging its head in embarrassment.

Maybe she was playing it cool until she sussed out why her

ex was back.

He wanted to believe it.

The realist in him said there was little else he could do for the moment than what he'd already offered to do for her. "I'll put the kettle on if you like when I'm done with the tree."

"Thanks, Graham." But her gaze was pinned on Lehman. "Hello, Malcolm. This is a surprise."

Lehman grinned. "I couldn't stay away."

As Graham walked past, Malcolm turned and spoke softly. "Don't let the door hit you on the way out."

"When you've gone, I'll park Janice's ute back where it belongs. If you happen to visit again, don't park in her spot. Ideally, don't come back."

Gauntlet thrown down.

He dropped Janice's pack inside for the time being and pulled the front door closed behind him. As he stepped off the veranda and headed down the side of the house, Janice was leaning against her ute, hands in her pockets, her eyes fixed on her ex.

She'd baked biscuits for Graham, not her ex.

Was he building hopes on a crumbling foundation? Or was their friendship nothing more than just friendship?

## Chapter 12

Cold seeped through Janice's jacket and the seat of her trousers as she leaned against the ute while her emotions whirled in an eddy of doubt, annoyance . . . hope . . .

Why did treacherous hope keep raising its head?

"Twice in two days, Malcolm? You must like the tea I serve." Sarcasm coloured the otherwise innocuous comment.

Once, she'd vowed before her family and God to love this man for better, for worse. Vows he'd turned his back on when he deserted her.

So why was he back now?

"Janice?" A note of pleading entered his voice. "I want us to be together. I'll keep coming back; I'll do whatever it takes until I prove to you—it *will* be different this time."

"I have no doubt you believe that, but in my experience, people don't change." The marriage counsellor had said much the same thing.

Malcolm bowed his head.

The unfamiliar action grated on her. Malcolm and contrition were strange bedfellows.

He tipped his head up just enough to make eye contact beneath hooded eyelids. Narrowed eyes, unblinking.

Once, she'd loved basking in his full attention.

This look was something else.

She wondered if this was what an animal felt like just before a snake struck.

She felt pinned like a butterfly in that awful lepidopterist display her grandfather had made. It sent a shiver down her spine.

Even his voice slithered. Snake-smooth. Hypnotic. "It isn't about me becoming different. People make mistakes. I made the biggest mistake of my life when I left you. I know I hurt you. I shouldn't have done that."

"Mistakes, regrets—we all have them, but some cut too deep to come back from."

He took a step towards her and one hand rose in entreaty. "Not us. Don't say it's impossible. We can come back from this. Please, Janey, forgive me?"

"No."

"You weren't so hard and cold when we were together. You preached kindness and compassion, forgiveness and putting the past behind us. Am I so undeserving of those things you hold dear?"

Malcolm hadn't lost his silver tongue.

Before, when they were married, nine times out of ten he'd win arguments, besting her by manipulating what she said, twisting it until she gave in, certain she was the one who'd been mistaken.

He had deliberately undermined her then.

She'd hated feeling like a victim, but the marriage

counsellor had helped her to deal with her self-doubt stemming from Malcolm's mental abuse.

"Don't put it back on me. You know what I value—*all* that I value." She took a step closer, her voice low and vehement. "I value keeping my word. When I give a promise, I keep it. What part of our marriage vows didn't you mean when you promised *'for better or worse and in sickness and health'*? When the worst came, you left. You threw away our life together. How am I now to blame for your choices?"

"I don't blame you, but why won't you give me another chance, give *us* another chance?"

"Why should I?" She folded her arms around her midriff.

"Janey, my love for you never died, but I—" His Adam's apple bobbed up and down and he half-turned and wiped his eyes. "When your last fertility treatment failed, I had a lot of anger in me. Instead of supporting you and exploring other options, I lashed out. Can you ever forgive me?"

Was that catch in his voice a sob?

Janice could feel herself weakening. Listening to him again. Letting him twist the facts to his own version.

Had she ever considered his feelings then, or had she been lost in a fog of despair?

Malcolm had always been proud—of his family name, and of his virility.

In the end their lovemaking had become desperate,

dwindling to nothing after the sorrow and despair of repeated failures—her failures—to fall pregnant.

The cold at her back spread through her body. On shaky legs, she walked towards him, stopping short of reaching out, of touching this man who had once been her world.

Malcolm took her hand in his, lifted it to his lips and kissed it. "Janey, can we at least try?"

Graham let the curtain fall over the loungeroom window. No words had filtered up to him, not with the hiss of the kettle in the background. But Lehman's body language spoke volumes. It smacked of triumph before he turned and followed Janice up the steps to the house.

Graham strode back into the kitchen and by the time the front door opened, he was clattering mugs and spoons onto a Chinese lacquered tray. "Water's almost boiling. What do you want to drink?"

"Coffee please. I'll be there in a moment to help, Graham. Just taking my boots off." Janice sat on the top step and unlaced her boots. Graham's were in the laundry out of respect for her 'no outside shoes inside' preference. He wriggled his toes in his socks, glad he'd put on his only non-holey pair this morning for breakfast with Anna and Jack.

Lehman walked into the room and sat, his shoes still on as he stretched his legs in front of him and crossed his ankles. "Any hope of decaf today?"

"Nope. Real coffee only. Janice doesn't like decaf."

"Janey," Lehman called through the doorway. "You always drank decaf when we were together."

Janice stepped into the loungeroom, her boots clenched in one hand, and closed the front door. "I prefer brewed coffee actually, or herbal tea at night. It was you who assumed I was content to drink your decaf and you who never let me buy the real stuff because you said you couldn't stand the smell. I no longer have to consider your preferences, Malcolm. We are divorced."

Her face was flushed, and she walked past Graham into the laundry.

Graham heard the clatter of her boots falling onto the floor, the rustle of her jacket as she hung it on its peg, followed by the sounds of her scrubbing her hands in the laundry sink.

Janice was disturbed about something and he had not one clue what had changed. He dumped a herbal teabag into a mug and splashed boiling water on top of it and set it to one side to brew. Carefully he measured freshly ground coffee and water into the coffee pot and set it to percolate.

He had no idea if Janice wanted him here. He wasn't sure whether to leave, or sit back and see how things unfolded.

"Is there a handtowel in here?" Janice stood in the laundry doorway, hands tipped up and dripping.

"Here." Graham grabbed the handtowel from where it hung

over the handle of the oven door and handed it to her.

"The cake is in the pantry, second-top shelf on the left. It's in a Tupperware container. Would you mind cutting some?"

"No worries. Janice—?"

"I'll be back soon. I need to wash my face."

She seemed brittle after her *tête-à-tête* with Lehman, as tightly strung as wire on a rabbit trap and as fragile as a dry gum leaf. Janice's high colour and glassy eyes suggested something had happened between them.

Graham took a half step back from the kitchen counter and checked on Lehman. The unwanted guest was leaning back with his hands behind his head as though he owned the place.

Janice hadn't asked Graham to leave. Whatever she was thinking, she had happily accepted his presence in her home while her ex-husband was visiting. Graham took what comfort he could from that.

By the time he carried the tray into the loungeroom and set it on the table—*been here, done this before*—Janice joined them, hair combed and her appearance neat.

Graham poured coffee into a mug and set it beside her, surreptitiously examining her face. Red rimmed her eyes and the tip of her nose was a little bit pink, but she'd lost the high colour that had flamed in her cheeks when she first came in. Had she retreated to the bathroom to cry?

He'd never have picked Janice as a crier. She was strong

and independent, and he was reasonably sure—he grimaced as the reality of thirty years living a bachelor life alone on a mountain mocked his certainty—that nothing he'd done had caused her red eyes.

It had to be something Lehman said or did.

Fuelled by anger, the same darkness that descended over him when a flashback hit threatened to cloud his mind. Graham felt it nudging at his self-control, threads of it wrapping around his freewill like black tentacles. Why was Janice sitting there making polite conversation with the lowlife?

Graham's breathing grew shallow.

He raced willy-nilly towards the darkness, wanting to embrace it, wanting to give in to it and unleash it on Lehman.

Short breaths, narrowed vision . . .

Darkness pressed in on all sides.

Control slipping away . . .

The scent of Janice as she reached past him . . .

Graham struggled to divert his thoughts to something pleasant, something non-confrontational. Losing it here in Janice's home wasn't an option. He had no idea if he might harm someone but breaking something was a given.

It would probably be Lehman's jaw.

Grinding his teeth, he tightened his grip on the coffee mug. Better that than Lehman's neck.

*Think of the bees. Imagine telling them you've taken a life.*

*No, no more killing. This isn't a war, and this isn't my battle. I've no right to do anything unless Janice asks for my help.*

"Graham? Sorry, I didn't catch what you said. Would you like a piece of cake?" Janice was standing in front of him, a fine china plate held out to him. On the plate lay a neat wedge of cake, something with vanilla and lemon. Gold rimmed the edge and red roses peeked out beneath the slice. Beside the cake rested a silver cake fork.

Had he ever in his life eaten cake with a cake fork?

The absurdity of it hit him in the gut. He clenched the tiny piece of cutlery in a work-roughened hand the size of a brick and achieved what all his visualisation hadn't managed. In his mind, he brandished this one small piece of silverware at the darkness in his mind and saluted as he imagined its retreat. With a sense of having achieved something momentous, he turned his back on his enemy.

*Today I win over you, darkness.*

"Yes please, Janice. I'd like a piece of cake."

## Chapter 13

There's a first time for everything.

Graham stared into the glowing embers deep in the heart of his campfire. A chorus line of flickering flames danced along a split log sitting on top of the embers. Victory was sweet, and vanquishing his dark beast warmed him, like the welcome buzzing of his bees. Other people called the beast their black dog, but his darkness was a dragon. It had teeth and claws and impregnable scales, and it had won every battle.

*Until today.*

*Do I imagine I'm Saint George?*

*A knight wielding a cake fork against a giant dragon.*

He chuckled at the image of himself as a knight.

At least he wasn't tilting at windmills like poor old Cervantes. But along with Jack's revelation over breakfast and today's victory, it had got him thinking. Maybe the need to control the darkness hadn't mattered enough before. Maybe he hadn't tried because there was nobody around to make the effort for.

Nobody cared if he lived or died.

But now there was Rick and, maybe one day unless Graham was very much mistaken, there would be Rick's children. For the first time in decades Graham had family.

He belonged.

For Rick, he had come down off his mountain.

For his future family, grandsons or granddaughters, he needed to get his shit together. It was useless to regret his failure to do so when he could have helped Alice, but it wasn't too late for Rick. It wasn't too late for the children he and Gei might have.

He wanted to be part of their lives.

But why had this first victory over his dragon happened when he was with Janice? It had nothing to do with outstaying Lehman this afternoon. Although that had felt pretty damned good, Graham's success had occurred earlier, before the man had started angling to stay the night.

And Janice wouldn't have a bar of him or his wheedling.

Sharp teacher tones telling him it wasn't appropriate had provoked an ugly glint in Lehman's eyes. Later, Graham had drawn Lehman's ire—and Janice's thanks after her ex had left—with his offer to start cooking dinner.

"Thanks Graham. There's mince in the fridge for that lasagne we talked about. I'll see Malcolm out."

Lehman's dirty look had bounced off Graham like the proverbial water off a duck's back. Why should he care that Janice's ex loathed the sight of him?

But one thing bothered him.

While Janice's back was turned as she opened the door and toed down a corner of the rug, Lehman had sent her a strange look, a look that had triggered a bad vibe in Graham's gut.

War had taught him something all right; it had taught him to notice the little things, the warning signs others missed or were oblivious to.

What was that look about?

Hours later he was still mulling over it. The why of it; the acquisitiveness in that look. Graham knew he hadn't imagined it. He'd be keeping an eye on Lehman until he left again—and Graham was sure he would.

Even if it meant more trips into town.

Strangely, the thought didn't turn his stomach. Why?

*And why can't I find the answer to that key question? Why did I beat back the darkness at Janice's and not when I was with Rick?*

Graham poured a couple of fingers from a bottle of the new batch of gin into a mug and corked the bottle. Alcohol had never become a crutch for him as it had for some of his comrades.

The attraction to him lay in the creative process, from initial idea to the careful measuring and blending of botanicals; these were the things he could control; things that brought him pleasure and a measure of peace.

He swirled the liquid and lifted it to his nose. Hints of lemon myrtle rose. He sipped, savoured, and nodded.

Tomorrow he'd take a bottle of this batch down to Rick at the winery. Together they would raise a glass to their business successes. But tonight—*tonight I'll toast my personal success. Here's to the beginning of change, of turning my life around. And all these questions?*

Tomorrow he'd go ask the bees.

Janice couldn't settle. Graham had insisted on cleaning up in the kitchen before he left. Wanting to offer him a lift, wondering if she dared kiss his cheek in farewell, she hesitated too long and he was gone.

She picked up the glass of gin and tonic he'd poured for her before he dried the last of the dishes and inhaled the scent. If she closed her eyes, the scent took her back to a very pleasant afternoon spent in Graham's company up on the hill. Rationing her drink to slow sips to put off the moment she'd head off to bed alone, she made it last until the heater switched off and the air grew too cool for comfort. Somewhere in the distance, a dog barked. She stood and listened. The dog barked again, a short yap and then, nothing.

Silence filled her loungeroom too. Silence was an absence of sound. How could an absence fill a space?

Nobody answered.

Shivering in the cool and lonely room, she looked from the sofa where Malcolm had sat to the armchair. It was easier to visualise Graham in her home than her ex-husband. Was it because with Graham she felt safe, comfortable, and something else, though precisely what she wasn't sure?

*He said I was easy to chat to.*

Maybe that was it. Graham had given her starved soul a meaningful compliment; one that, coming from a quiet man like him, meant something. Perhaps it was only that Graham had stayed here briefly when she was sick. They'd shared meals and he'd guided her shaky steps to the bathroom.

Malcolm had never lived here, never set foot inside until he'd turned up so unexpectedly. He'd made no imprint in this house. It was hers, and hers alone.

No shared experiences, no history of them together.

Malcolm would have scoffed at this rental she'd moved into after their property settlement.

She put the glass in the sink and turned off the lights. Feeling her way along the dim hall, she closed the door of her bedroom. In the far corner, the timer switch on her heater ticked, counting down the minutes until it turned off for the night.

Counting down the minutes of her life.

Bustling into the bathroom, she attacked her nightly routine with energy, as though the activity could fill the lonely night with meaning and purpose. But with each stroke of the brush through her hair, one question played, over and over.

Why had Malcolm come back now?

## Chapter 14

Sunlight touched the beehives, warming the wood beneath Graham's fingers. An overnight frost and crisp clear morning had turned into one of those soft winter days that made him glad to be alive.

He set out sugar water and filled shallow pans with salty water. Daytime temperatures were still warm enough for his bees to be active, but the wintertime chore relaxed him and kept the bees fed now flowers were scarce.

He slipped his hand into the back handhold and lifted the first hive. It was a good weight. He moved on, checking the rest of the hives, pleased to find them in good health. Less than five per cent loss over winter was excellent and it looked like his autumn preparations were paying off. A touch of pride mingled with contentment. If the other hives closer to the creek were in as good condition, next spring he planned to add beeswax candles to what he sent to market.

Did Jaz, Freda Moloney's granddaughter who sold his honey alongside her family's cheeses at the market stalls, ever wonder about the source of Wild Ridge Honey? Would she be curious if candles starting turning up with the crate of honey each market day?

Graham stepped on a fallen branch and skidded a short way

down the slope. He needed to stop daydreaming and pay attention. If he had an accident up here, no one would find him for days.

He'd rarely let that thought worry him. In the early days he would have welcomed such pain as his penance for the lives he'd taken in Afghanistan. Nothing had seemed too dangerous or off-limits when he might offer his pain as atonement. If he'd died up here, who would care? Who would mourn?

*There wouldn't have been anyone to tell the bees that I was gone.*

But now there was Rick.

And Janice. Somehow the schoolteacher had got under his guard. He liked her, and he thought she liked him. Enough to bake for him.

And enough to welcome him to her home for dinner next week even after their spontaneous dinner last night, he thought.

Dinner without her ex-husband, although he doubted the lack of an invitation would stop Malcolm Lehman.

Graham took more care negotiating the steep slope down to the creek hives. He'd named one of the queens Cleopatra and Lark Creek was her Nile River. The idea amused him, and he whistled a snatch of one of Alice's favourite songs as he approached the cleared stretch of bank where his hives nestled into the north-east facing slope.

It was the buzzing of the bees that sent a rush of adrenaline surging through his body. Unusual for this time of year. Unusual and agitated.

Instinct and caution silenced his steps as he circled through the trees that ringed the clearing. Approaching from the other side he'd have the advantage of the sun behind him and in the eyes of whoever or whatever was upsetting the bees.

He stopped beside a black wattle and scanned ahead. A slice of the clearing opened before him—the first of his hives, a shimmer of sunlight on the water—peaceful, as it should be, except for the angry buzzing.

He stepped around the wattle.

The second to last hive was on the ground. Hard up against its base lay a body.

Bees disturbed from their fallen hive flitted in tight random circuits around their home and the intruder. The dead man lay on his back, sightless eyes staring at the bright winter sky. From his chest, a knife protruded.

Careful not to get too close so any physical evidence was preserved, Graham stepped sideways in a semi-circle until he was looking directly at the body.

The knife was embedded almost to its hilt.

*Murder, not suicide.*

Graham sank onto his haunches. He'd seen too much death for this one to make him puke and yet his gut roiled.

The knife in the dead man's chest was his.

"Did you touch the body or the knife before you called us?" Constable Marion Brooks stood beside Graham, her back to the police photographer capturing details of the crime scene and the body. Probably this was her first homicide. She looked a bit green around the gills but pressed on with her questions.

Graham couldn't change the fact the man was dead, and near his hives. It was simply fact. He'd deal with it. Had dealt with it as far as he was concerned.

The tension he'd felt tightening like a screw inside him eased a little. He'd done the right things, hadn't messed up the scene, called the police. "No."

The constable's eyebrows rose, eloquent in their disbelief. "You didn't go over to check he was dead?"

He refrained from letting sarcasm tint his tone. The constable hadn't thrown up, but the sight of this murder had rattled her. It would sicken most people. "Did *you* think he might still be alive when you first saw him?"

She sucked in a quick breath and glanced back at the body. Definitely rattled.

"Point taken. You're ex-military, aren't you, Mr Peyton?"

"SAS, Afghanistan. Yes, that's my knife, yes, I know how to wield it, and no, I didn't kill him."

The constable was silent for a handful of heartbeats and then, "Do you know who he was?"

"I've never seen him before. I found him, left the scene

undisturbed and walked to the nearest house to call you."

"Why didn't you call us on your mobile?"

"Don't own one. Never have."

Constable Brooks closed her notebook, her gaze drawn like a magnet to the body. She flinched, looked away, and drew in an audible, slightly shaky breath.

"Is this your first dead body?" he asked.

Her gaze came back to his and he could read her answer in her eyes before she replied. "No, my second. The first time I threw up. How do you . . ." Her question trailed into nothingness and she pressed her lips together. "Sorry, I shouldn't ask."

Graham folded his arms. Later, he knew this morning's fatal discovery would come back at him with ferocious intent.

Every body he'd even seen did that.

Later, when he lay down to sleep, he would battle his dragon, but for the moment, he clamped a lid on other memories crawling around the edge of his mind as they tried to escape.

"I can't say it gets easier." Graham looked at the police officer, his voice gruff, but gentle. "But maybe the shock is less when you understand what you're seeing. When you've seen death more times than anyone wants to, this familiarity doesn't mean you will ever accept the finality of it, or the brutality of some deaths. But it does let you respond more—clinically. It is possible to detach yourself from the horror and indecency of what man commits on another human being so you can seek justice."

The police photographer approached. "I'm done. Is it okay for these guys to take the body now?"

"I'll check with the senior sergeant." Constable Brooks turned back to Graham. "Thank you. What you said—well, that will help me next time. Everybody deserves justice."

He watched as she walked over to Tony Edwards and cleared the removal of the body with her superior officer. The senior sergeant nodded and signalled his agreement to the men waiting a little way off from the scene.

They moved in and loaded the body into a recovery pod.

Edwards watched until the body disappeared from view, and then looked at Graham, a look that sent a cold sweat trickling down his spine.

Edwards had long detested Rick. Despite proof to the contrary, the police sergeant apparently believed there was substance to the rumour that Rick must have known about his stepfather's illegal drug kitchen.

Edwards strolled over and stepped into Graham's personal space. Intimidation tactics aside, it was obvious he wanted to rub in the difficulty of the situation Graham found himself in. "Looks like all the Peytons are tarred with the same brush."

*Don't rise to the bait.* He kept his trap shut and met the policeman's eyes.

"I don't believe in coincidences. Your story is cock and bull. Do you expect me to believe you just happened to stumble over a body that happened to have your knife in its chest? Give me a break. You think you can get away with this, well let me tell you—you won't."

"I'll tell my lawyer what you think."

"You do that, but if you're guilty I will get you, Peyton, and I will put you where you belong. Four walls and a barred window. You won't roam these hills again—ever."

Susanne Bellamy

## Chapter 15

Janice parked in front of the newsagents and checked the time. She'd made it with five minutes to spare. Slamming the car door, she glanced at the front door of the shop. Good, Gary hadn't flipped the closed sign over yet, but Kendall, the Grade three teacher, was peering intently at an information wanted poster taped to the inside of the sliding door.

Janice stepped across the deep bluestone kerbing. She'd never seen any of the young teachers in the newsagent's shop. They sent electronic cards and read the news online and were probably part of why Gary had reduced his floor space to half of its former area.

She stopped beside her colleague, unable to open the door without interrupting whatever had the young woman so interested. "Hello. How's your weekend going?"

Kendall jumped and her hand slapped against her chest. "Oh hi, Janice. You gave me a fright."

"Sorry. What are you looking at?"

"This poster. Marion Brooks just put it up." Wind gusted down the street and she stuck her hands into the pocket of her jeans.

Janice looked at the image. "There's something unnaturally still about that man's face. I wonder why his eyes are closed?"

"Maybe he's dead. The caption asks if anyone has seen him or knows who he is to contact the police. Gosh, I wonder if something's happened in sleepy old Lark Creek?"

The edge of excitement in Kendall's voice made Janice feel queasy.

How could anyone get excited over the idea of someone being found dead in their town?

"I'm sorry for anyone who knows him in that case. Imagine how awful they would feel if this is how they find out their son or brother or friend is dead."

Kendall's mouth opened and closed, and embarrassed heat coloured her face. "Oh, I didn't think of that. You don't know him, do you?"

"No, but someone in town might. And if the man is dead, seeing this will be a real shock. Do you mind if I just nip inside and then you can keep reading?"

"Sure. Sorry." She stepped to the side.

Janice tugged the heavy sliding door along its track and pulled it closed behind her. "How are you, Gary? Glad I caught you."

Gary dropped the magazine he'd been reading, pushed his spectacles up and sat them on top of his balding head and smiled. "I wondered if I'd see you today."

"You know me well. Has that new John Grisham book come in yet?"

"You must be psychic. I was going to email you when I closed up today. It came in this morning's delivery."

"I don't know about psychic, but I do need some distraction. Don't worry about wrapping it. I'll just slip it into my bag."

"Right you are. It's out the back. Actually, would you flip the closed sign for me please? I won't be long."

"Sure." Janice took her wallet from her shoulder bag and turned towards the door. A pair of jeans-clad legs was visible through the glass, but the upper body was hidden by the poster and other notices. Why was Kendall still reading that notice? Had she remembered seeing the man in town?

The figure swayed and Janice realised it wasn't Kendall on the other side of the door. Malcolm was standing outside where she'd seen her colleague.

Was he waiting for her?

She strode to the door and pulled it open with a little too much force. It flew along the track and banged when it hit the metal stopper. "I don't want you following me around town. It's too much . . ." Words deserted her as she looked at Malcolm's pale face and pinched lips.

"Malcolm? What's the matter?"

His eyes flickered from her to the poster and he cleared his throat, the sound too loud and nervous, unnatural in a man who was always so sure of himself.

Comprehension dawned on Janice and her comment to Kendall roared back.

*Imagine how awful if this is how they find out . . .*

"Do you know the man in the poster?"

Malcolm blinked and slowly shook his head. His voice when it emerged was thin, a scaled back whisper of itself. "Never seen him before."

"Then why do you look like you've seen a ghost?" Such a cliché, but something had shattered his usual confidence.

Malcolm's throat bobbed up and down, he coughed and, finally, met her gaze. "I suddenly felt dizzy. Nothing to do with the poster."

She didn't believe him.

If she was being brutally honest, something had rattled her ex-husband. If not the man in the poster, was he suffering some sort of breakdown?

"Wait there." She touched his shoulder.

He nodded.

She raced inside, paid Gary with cash and a quick "thanks" and shoved her new book into her bag.

Malcolm was leaning against the brick wall right where she'd left him.

She took his arm and steered him down the street towards the pub.

Was his *turn* no more than a tactic to win her sympathy?

He'd been a master at manipulating her emotions when they were married. With each step she berated herself for caving in. Why hadn't she led him straight to the doctor's surgery?

Pity, leftover feelings, and the fact the surgery was closed; all were reason enough to be doing this.

In a quiet corner of the dining lounge in the pub, she pushed him onto a seat and watched for any sign of physical distress. "I'll get you a drink. Whisky?"

"Brandy. Straight. Double."

"Stay there." Within two minutes she set a glass in front of Malcolm. Fifteen minutes later and Wes behind the bar would have been busy with early pre-dinner drinkers.

Malcolm picked up the brandy and swallowed half in one gulp and wiped his mouth on the back of his hand.

Janice stared, shocked. Another first.

Malcolm was fastidious. He believed in sipping in a civilised manner, not sculling a drink.

"What? I needed that."

She leaned back in her chair. "You're welcome. Are you going to tell me what that was about?"

"Nothing to tell. I saw you in the shop. I was going to come in, but then I had a bit of a turn."

"Has it happened before? Have you seen a doctor?"

"No need. I'm fine. Stop fussing, woman." Nothing of his glib comments or silver tongue—which reinforced her feeling that he'd suffered a shock of some kind. Could it have been a turn like he said?

Perhaps he was telling the truth. That awful pallor had gone and colour was returning to his cheeks.

He raised the glass and sipped. "Life isn't the same without you, Janey. Have you been thinking about us?"

"It's hard not to when you're on my doorstep all the time. Tell me what's changed." She held up a hand to stop the obvious answer, the one he'd given her last time. "And don't tell me you made a mistake again. I don't want to hear it."

Malcolm gave her the wounded look, a look he had down to a tee. "That's not kind. That's not the Janey I used to know."

"That's just it, Malcolm. I am no longer that person, and don't call me Janey. My name is Janice."

"You'll always be my Janey."

"We are divorced. Our differences were irreconcilable, remember? Clearly, we never knew each other as well as we thought we did when we were living together. What makes you think you know me any better now?"

"We loved each other, and we made vows to look after each other."

"I kept my vows."

"And so did I."

"Running off like you did isn't keeping your vows."

They should have talked like this before he left. Why

hadn't they ever talked things through? She'd even attended marriage-counselling sessions alone after Malcolm refused point blank to go.

"True, I failed when you needed me most. But Janey, did you ever think, in all we went through, that I needed you. That you weren't there for me either."

Bam!

He'd never hurled that stone at her in the bleak days after the last treatment failed. As hurt as he was, he'd held back on that complaint.

Not even her Catholic upbringing would have saved her if he'd hurled that weapon.

Had Malcolm recognised that about her, even from the depths of his own sadness? Was there a skerrick of honour left in him, she wondered?

Lost in her grief, unaware of anything beyond her broken dreams, she hadn't considered how he was feeling. But he had understood that accusation would have tipped her over the edge.

"You're saying I failed you?" It was a tough question to ask, but she needed to know. Lashing out, blaming Malcolm for the breakdown of their marriage had been too easy. Where did the truth lie?

"We failed each other. We're human. Isn't this reason enough to try again? Janey, I need you."

There it was again—Malcolm's first person singular focus.

It stiffened her resolve to hang on to her newfound and hard-won self-sufficiency.

Maybe she hadn't been there for him, but she'd barely been able to stay above water in the ocean of her own loss and grief.

It always came back to this same point.

They had both failed this supreme test of their marriage.

*He left and I moved on.*

Father Mulroney had had a great deal to say in the weeks after Malcolm left. Oh, as expected, he'd had plenty to say about God's will. "The answer to your prayers is sometimes no, Janice."

That had been hardest of all to take.

But despite encouraging her to forgive her husband for leaving, she'd appreciated the priest's support. And she had eventually moved on.

Janice bit back a sigh. "But Malcolm, I don't need you. I'm self-sufficient and I enjoy doing what I want, when I want. I don't have to cook if I don't feel like it, and I can sleep in the extra half an hour because I don't have to be out of the bathroom so you can take your sweet time getting that close shave you like."

Malcolm stared at her as if he'd never seen her before—and maybe he hadn't.

"You sound like you hate me?"

"No, not hate. I don't even dislike you now, but—"

"Janey, how could you dislike me? We had twenty great years together."

Did we?"

"You know we did. You kept my name."

"I know that when you left I—" She couldn't continue. Emotion clogged her throat. Anger, fear, crushing self-doubt . . . and a terrible grief. They weren't buried as deep as she'd thought. Playing for time, praying for divine guidance, she sipped her drink.

"Forgive him, Janice. To forgive is divine and bestows grace on the giver." Father Mulroney's counsel had been tough love and she'd needed it.

*I have forgiven him for some things. But . . .*

"I loved you once, Malcolm, but I'm no longer in love with you."

His eyes narrowed and he gripped her free hand where it rested on the table between them. The grip was tight, meant to make a statement. "It's because of that Peyton fellow. I've lost you to the hermit."

"I'm not a possession for you to lose." She pulled her hand free and glanced around, not relishing the thought of becoming gossip fodder with yet another man.

Malcolm seemed to deflate.

Her tart tones and a flicker of anger in her voice—had they finally registered with him? Was he was finally listening to her?

His shoulders hunched and he stared into his glass. "I didn't mean it like that."

"Then how did you mean it?" She softened her tone. While

it was heady, this feeling of being in control, she didn't intend to inflict hurt on Malcolm. But she wouldn't allow him to back her into an emotional corner ever again.

What was it the marriage counsellor had said? *You need to take back power and rebalance your relationship.*

Malcolm had made most of the decisions in their marriage and she'd allowed that to happen. Maybe in this she'd been at fault.

Her choice to get counselling had been too little, too late.

Had she been too agreeable when they were married?

"How could you have taken up with someone like him?"

Malcolm's question drew her attention back to the present.

"Graham's a kind and caring and decent man who chooses to live life on his terms. Any woman would be lucky to—"

He held up a hand.

Force of habit—twenty years worth of habit—stopped her flow of words.

"I get it. Please don't make me keep apologising for leaving you. I was wrong to go."

Janice broke eye contact. She didn't want to have this conversation here. She didn't want to have this conversation at all, but Malcolm wasn't going anywhere until he'd said his piece. And perhaps it was past time they had a soul-baring conversation. Clearing the anger and hurt of their past could lead both of them into happier futures.

Just not with each other.

Dealing with the past would be so much easier if she knew exactly what she wanted. Once, it had been Malcolm and no other.

But what about her new friendship with Graham?

People were arriving for dinner and casting blatantly interested looks their way. It was up to her to put a stop to speculation by leaving. She pushed her chair back from the table and picked up her handbag.

"Don't go." A flash of fear darted through his eyes.

Fear? That was crazy.

"What is it you want from me, Malcolm?"

"Give me a chance? That's all I'm asking for."

Janice tossed and turned and finally—with the clock showing it was 3.37 in the morning—sat up in bed. Sleep wasn't coming, her head ached, and she wondered how, once again, Malcolm had got his way.

Broken snores filtered through the wall and down the hallway from the lounge.

How had Malcolm conned her into letting him stay at her home? Had it been his "the pub's so noisy I can't sleep", or was it the repeated references to his dizzy spell this afternoon and how special were the wedding vows that they'd made?

"Can I stay with you, for old times' sake, Janey? It would be awful to have another turn when I'm alone. Just for tonight?"

Giving in was what she'd always done with Malcolm. Letting him have his way was the path of least resistance, but now, with his snoring growing more strident and her tolerance deep diving, annoyance grew. Annoyance churned her stomach, made her head throb and sent her stress levels soaring.

Tomorrow she would tell him that he had to move back into town. She'd hate anyone to think we're back together.

Anyone?

She flicked her bedside lamp on and tugged the doona up under her chin.

She'd hate it if Graham were to stop visiting. And she'd told him their dinner would be just the two of them. What if he saw Malcolm's car parked here and assumed things had changed?

That thought really did churn the little she'd managed to eat of dinner.

It seemed the mountain man had got under her skin after all.

## Chapter 16

Graham sat on a log in front of his campfire, stirring the ashes. A chunk of charred wood slipped through the metal grate.

Four walls and a barred window . . .

"You'll never roam these hills again . . ."

An empty threat—it had to be. There was no proof because he was innocent and yet . . .

He glanced up through the branches. A sliver of ridge thrust skywards, the point he'd chosen if he ever needed to end it all. If Edwards fabricated evidence; if somehow the worst happened and he couldn't escape, there was always that choice.

If it came to that.

Police officers had searched his campsite for most of the afternoon and dug up several patches of ground deemed to be of interest. They'd found nothing, but they'd left one hell of a mess. Even the campfire had been scattered and the ashes searched, and it had been all he could do to convince them not to open up the hives. Only the implied threat of multiple bee stings had stopped them. That, and Marion Brooks' suggestion of bringing in a bee specialist.

"Don't leave the district," Marion Brooks had told him with a little quirk of the lips. Tony Edwards had just scowled. Probably champing at the bit to make a case against him. Being a *person of interest* sucked, big time.

Graham cleaned out the fireplace and got the fire going again. Rumbling in his stomach reminded him he'd missed lunch. It would be a while before the newly set fire was hot enough to cook dinner. Right now, all he wanted was a mug of tea laced with something alcoholic. Enough to take the edge off his worst nightmare.

Did everyone in Lark Creek know about his claustrophobia?

Damn him, Edwards knew how to hit below the belt.

He zoned out into that nightmare and the first he knew of Rick's approach was when his son stopped beside him, his gaze searching Graham's face.

"Dad, I just heard what happened. Are you okay?"

Graham stood and wiped his hands on his behind. "I'm fine. Can't say the same for my camp."

Rick's glance moved from fire to tent to the piles of dirt where someone hadn't filled in a hole they'd dug. "Did the cops do this? Edwards is an incompetent blowhard."

"My knife was found in a dead body on my bit of the mountain. Reckon he had cause to search."

"Search, maybe, but this?" Anger set a fire in his son's gaze and burned red in his face. "Come down and eat dinner with us."

"Tempting, but I need to tidy up."

"I'll give you a hand and then we'll go. Gei's expecting you."

"In that case can you collect my tools and stack them in the corner?"

Dinner had been relaxed, with an overlay of extra effort by Gei to keep the conversation light. Two things from the evening stood out in Graham's mind as he strode back up the hill, leftovers tucked under his arm in a cooler pack. Both were surprising, in a good way.

The first was how much he enjoyed time spent with family. Having spent so many years alone and self-sufficient in everything, the simple pleasure of good company with people he wanted to be with was still a revelation.

The second positive was promising for the changes he had decided to make if he was going to play a role within his small family. They'd not only eaten dinner in the dining room, but when Gei slipped on a heavy jacket and picked up the tray to take their coffee onto the veranda, he'd stopped her. "I'm fine to stay inside for coffee. It's too cold out there for you."

Eyes wide, Gei looked at Rick.

He shook his head. "Seems like your time caring for Janice has a side benefit." Rick grinned but didn't pursue it further as he took the tray from Gei, set it down on the table, and poured filter coffee into three cups.

Maybe Rick was right. Circumstances had forced Graham to subdue his phobia in order to care for Janice. Maybe gradual exposure to what caused his problem was the answer?

He doubted it would it be as simple as that, but maybe it was past time to talk to someone, to a professional.

He reached the lower slopes and passed a surveyor's marker glowing ghostly in the moonlight. Would Jack have any news about the developer this week?

Angling up the slope towards his camp, Graham began making a mental list for the coming week: check the creek beehives when the police were finished with the crime scene, dinner with Janice—if Jacky was laying, he could make a wattle seed cake to take—see Jack about the developer and finding a therapist, sourcing wicks for the beeswax candles . . .

And keeping a low profile while Edwards conducted his investigation.

Clouds scudded across the moon. The soft light disappeared, and the trees darkened into dark grey smudges against the black. The air was cool, the wind brisk, and his camp was no more than a hundred metres away when light and movement ahead caught his eye.

Torchlight, carefully shaded, made a small circle of light through the trees, more noticeable in the moonless dark.

Whoever was there, they must be near one of the markers.

Graham lowered the cooler bag, feeling his way down the closest tree trunk and setting the cooler bag between two side roots. Keeping an eye on the torchlight, he stepped noiselessly along the invisible track, climbing by instinct.

As cold as the night was, the uninvited guests were probably nothing more than a young couple making out.

But after this morning, he wasn't about to assume anything.

"Attack from the high ground, defend from the heights." The drill sergeant's voice was as clear and fresh as if he was back in basic training.

Using the terrain had been drilled into him, and he was on home turf. Any incursion on his patch would be treated as suspicious until he learned otherwise.

At last he reached a spot from where he could look down on the intruder. A lone dark-clad figure had lifted one of the markers and was digging beneath it. As Graham watched, he—*I think it's a male*—lowered something into the hole and sat back on his heels. Panted breaths sounded harsh in the quiet night.

At a distance down on Ridge Road, a car engine grew louder, and a pair of headlights cut a double path of light in their direction. One of the Donovan vehicles turned onto the track up to the house.

The light was nowhere near the digger, but he dropped to the ground and remained there until the headlights went out and a car door slammed.

Distant as the farm was, the man's reaction made it clear that, whatever he was doing, he didn't want anyone to know he was here.

Which meant he was up to no good.

Graham waited and watched as the hole was filled in and the marker set back in place. It was obvious to him the ground had been disturbed, but would anyone else notice, or would they think it was nothing more than dirt from the insertion of the marker?

Not many people came up this far, and of those who did, few would pay attention to the white markers. To them, the markers were minor visual pollution, skimmed over as the eye took in vistas of valley and ridge. To Graham, the markers were imbued with sinister intent.

Marker—digger—dead man.

He watched and waited as the digger filled in the hole and pushed the marker in.

Was it possible the digger with his secret stash had killed the murdered man? The digging on top of the murder couldn't be coincidence.

So where did that leave him?

Graham followed the man at a discreet distance across the top of the meadow above Dawnie Farm, through a stand of beech trees on the western boundary of Jack and Anna's place and lost him on the far side. Graham turned down towards Ridge Road, certain he'd find his quarry heading for a parked vehicle some distance away.

An engine sparked to life behind him, someone dropped a gear and spun their wheels as they roared off in the opposite direction.

Damn, he hadn't expected the man to escape on a trail bike along the dirt track that led west. But the exit route made it less likely the intruder was a local.

That opened up a whole new set of possibilities.

An outside security light flicked on at Cottage Farm, spotlighting Jack emerging from the woodshed, a pile of wood in one arm as he crossed the yard.

"Yo, Jack, it's Graham." He slipped through the wire strands of the back fence and walked towards the cottage.

"Graham, you're out late. Anything wrong?"

"Could be. Got a moment?"

"Come on in. I got home late from court in Dalton and Anna wasn't thrilled to find the wood box empty when she got home late too. Coffee?"

"Thanks." He sat on the top step and removed his shoes and then entered and sat at the kitchen table facing the window. "Might be a good thing you have the security lights and cameras in place."

Jack dusted off wood splinters from his jacket into a replica coal scuttle that held wood for the kitchen range and hung his jacket on the back of a chair. "Anna loves using the wood stove in winter. What's happened?"

In succinct, sterile sentences, while Jack made coffee and set it on the table, Graham shared the day's events right up to losing the intruder behind Jack's place. "That's it. I don't have evidence; just a gut feeling that whatever he dropped into that hole must be connected to the dead body."

Jack nodded. "I have to be cautious in my work about how I connect the dots, but I'm with you. Something's going on here, and it's dangerous. If that dead man is linked to whatever your intruder buried, we've got to find out what it is, and quickly. Who knows how long it will be before someone comes to retrieve it?"

"I've got spades back at camp."

"We'll take mine. It'll be quicker." Jack tossed back the last of his coffee and stood.

A soft footfall alerted Graham to Anna's arrival a moment before she spoke. "Hello, Graham. Where might you be taking Jack off to in the middle of the night?"

She stood in the doorway, a thick green dressing gown and messy hair suggesting she'd been in bed.

"Anna, um . . ." He didn't want to scare her. Heaven knew, Anna was a brave woman and she'd proven it over and over in the past year. Caring for Kaden in witness protection had been no picnic. Nor was escaping over the ridge in the dark of night.

But he didn't want to scare her with a dead body almost on her doorstep.

"We—I—that is—" Dissembling didn't come naturally to him. Come to that, neither did small talk. He looked to Jack for help.

Grinning, Anna came towards him and put a hand on his arm. "It's okay, Graham. Tell me when you're able to. Just—keep an eye out for Jack."

"I can take care of myself." Jack sounded mildly amused.

Anna slipped her arms around Jack's waist and kissed his mouth. "I know you can, but Graham knows the ridge and—other stuff. Just tell me one thing, does where you're going have anything to do with the body Graham found this morning?"

Graham narrowed his gaze. *She's too smart to miss the connection.*

Jack dropped a kiss on her head. "Maybe, but we've really got no idea until we dig up what somebody buried near Graham's campsite."

"Then off you go. My bed is calling, unless there's anything you want me to do?"

"Nothing, but thanks." Jack kissed her and then shrugged into his jacket.

Graham sat on the top step and laced his boots. "Are you happy for me to get the spade?"

"Go ahead, the shed isn't locked, but grab the torch from the wall. There's no electricity in the shed."

Security lights made Graham's walk to the shed easy.

Inside the windowless building was a different story. Graham switched the torch on, startling a possum mother and baby. The pair scurried through a narrow space between roof and wall, leaving behind fresh droppings and the smell of possum, pungent in the confined space.

Graham grabbed two spades and pulled the door closed behind him just as Jack appeared around the corner. "All set."

Torch off, with only the faint spill of moonlight escaping from behind a bank of clouds to guide them, they slipped through the gate between Cottage Farm and Dawnie, keeping to the fence line and using the deep cover of the trees until they reached the top meadow. The moon rose and its light bathed the meadow in silver. They waited beneath an old oak.

Open country with unknown adversaries chasing unknown goals was a bad idea.

At last, heavy clouds rolled through hiding the moon and stars. The wind rose, chill and carrying the scent of river and bush.

"There'll be rain before morning." Graham spoke softly. "Let's go."

With the torchlight on its lowest setting and angled low, just ahead of their feet, they jogged across the open ground.

When they reached the tree cover on the lower slope of the ridge they slowed, but on the way to the marker, Graham's senses were on high alert. Keen night vision was no match for a man with a night scope.

Was he being overly cautious? Seeing danger everywhere?

Or was he simply preparing for the worst?

He couldn't dismiss the coincidence. In that respect he agreed with Sergeant Edwards. The thought gave him cold comfort.

When they reached the marker, he stood to one side and scanned the area.

Jack waited, his breathing only slightly elevated from the run. "Damned if I can see anything. It's black as ink."

"You were looking at the torchlight."

"Of course I was. I didn't want to step in a rabbit hole. Are you telling me you weren't?"

"One of us needed to preserve our night vision. Looks like it's clear for the moment." He set the spades on the ground.

"Anna was right. You've got some seriously mad survival skills."

"Whatever it is, it's buried under this one. Shine the torch here." He reached for the marker. Wiggling it was easy. Whoever had filled the hole had done a sloppy job of repositioning the marker. It came out of with a couple of hefty tugs and Graham tossed it aside. "He didn't stop to hammer the marker in, which makes me think whatever he buried wasn't meant to be here for long."

Jack picked up one of the spades. "Or he didn't want anyone to hear him. My turn. Hold this." He handed the torch to

Graham and pushed the spade into lightly packed earth, turning it out and beginning a side pile of dirt. Reddish-brown and freshly dug, it came out in clumps; several rolled down the growing pile of dirt and one kept going downhill.

Keeping the torchlight trained on the growing hole, Graham continued scanning the area below.

*All quiet.*

He felt the whoosh of wings over his head and ducked before he caught the flash of an owl diving, and the cut off squeak of its prey.

"What was that?" Jack had ducked too and now stood with the spade raised over his shoulder, poised and ready to resist attack.

"Owl out hunting. He caught his dinner."

"Sheesh, and I thought it would be quiet living up here." He blew out a breath and pushed the spade into the deepening hole.

"Nights can seem noisier than days. When it's dark and everything is settling down to sleep, I hear the night creatures."

"How do you sleep?" Jack pushed the spade in again and stopped, lifted it a little and tapped it lightly over one spot. "Shine the torch here. I felt something."

Graham squatted at the edge of the hole and directed the beam at the tip of the spade. He reached in and flicked dirt off what appeared to be the top of a feed bag. Setting the torch on the side of the hole, he scooped with his hands and brushed dirt off the bag until he could get a solid grip and then tugged.

It came free and dirt cascaded from the edges into the bottom of the hole.

He set the bag down and met Jack's gaze. "Shall I do the honours?"

"Yeah, put me out of my misery."

Graham took care with the unwrapping, memorising the folds on the off chance they decided they needed to bury it again. Inside the bag was a metal toolbox. "It isn't locked." He wiped his fingers on his trousers and flicked the catches up.

Inside the toolbox was a sealed plastic bag.

"Whatever this is, it's got enough layers to withstand a flood." Graham opened the last layer. Inside lay a thick blue manila folder, similar to those he'd seen on Jack's office desk.

"Don't touch it." Jack's comment whipped out and his hand stopped Graham's from picking up the folder.

"Why? Don't you want to know what the hell's going on?"

"Yes, but I've got a bad feeling about this."

"Because of the murder this morning?"

"Yes. It was your knife found in the body. What if that— and this—is a set up?"

The thought hadn't occurred to Graham. It sure as hell wouldn't occur to Sergeant Edwards. He would see Graham's fingerprints as an admission of guilt if what was in the folder was linked to the murdered man. "I assumed it was an opportunistic theft from my campsite. You know I didn't kill that bloke, right?"

"I know. But your knife was used as a murder weapon, and the same night, very close to your campsite, you see someone bury something. What if you were meant to see him? The natural thing is to dig up what was buried."

"And then my fingerprints would be all over it, literally. Shit."

## Chapter 17

Jack reached for the toolbox and held out his hand for the plastic wrapped bundle. "Let's take it back to the cottage. Anna's washing up gloves should do the trick."

"You've just added your fingerprints to mine."

"Yes. If we have to turn this over to the police, I want it very clear that I was here with you."

"Edwards won't believe you."

"I doubt Edwards' pay grade will be up to whatever's going on. Besides, I can always call Smithy if push comes to shove with Edwards."

Graham pressed his fingers against his temple. Edwards' threat throbbed like a primal drumbeat in his head. He couldn't go to jail.

Jack handed him a spade, took the bag and set it down out of the way. "We'll fill in the hole and then get the hell out of here. Grab anything you need from your camp and stay the night in the cottage."

Graham tipped a load of dirt into the hole. "No, I won't bring trouble to your doorstep."

"We're not strangers to trouble, and anyway, you saved Anna and Kaden. I'd say we're in your debt."

"There is no debt. Besides, it's not just you in that house, and Anna doesn't deserve to be put in danger again."

"Assuming we aren't seeing bogeymen, yes, there might be danger, but I'm betting Anna will agree."

"Probably. That's why I won't put you in that position." Graham changed his stance and dragged dirt in angry jerks into the hole. It filled quickly.

"On your theory of not bringing trouble to our home, that wipes out everyone you know—Rick and Gei, Janice—"

"Enough, Jack. I haven't lived for thirty years up here without learning how to take care of myself."

It was well after midnight by the time they set the bundle on the kitchen table in Cottage Farm. Jack eased the door into the lounge closed before turning on the light. "I'm hoping Anna stays asleep."

"Her dreams will be better if she doesn't know about this." Already he was regretting involving Jack. If there was a target on his back, the further away he stayed from everyone, the better.

"Do you mind if I open it?" Jack patted the bundle.

*Do I mind? If someone's targeting me, I mind a whole damn lot.* "I think I should."

Jack took a pair of rubber washing up gloves off the metal draining board and held them up. "I don't think Anna's gloves will fit your hands."

"They won't fit yours either."

"I have a better chance of getting them on than you do." Jack set one hand on the table beside Graham's.

"Point taken. I have big hands."

Jack pulled the gloves on and held both hands up in front of him. "Ready to open." He sat on the chair facing Graham and, for the second time that evening they unwrapped the folder.

He set aside each layer until the blue folder lay on the table. Carefully he opened it. A bundle of one hundred-dollar notes wrapped in a thick rubber band lay on top of photos and papers. Jack picked up the bundle and blanched, his Adam's apple bobbing up and down.

Even upside down, Graham felt his own gorge rise at what lay below. "Reckon that's the murder young Kaden witnessed. Cops found the body. Why would anyone think that photo needs to be kept secret?"

Jack cleared his throat and turned the obscene photo over. He examined the second photo. "Maybe because this one shows the murderer caught in the act. And it isn't Ferdy Hickman. I'm calling Smithy now."

Smithy sat back in the chair and cradled a mug of steaming coffee. The Federal investigator eyed off Graham and Jack and shook his head. "You have an amazing talent for being in the wrong place at the wrong time, Jack, and you too, Graham."

"I'd say it's more, right place and time. What else was in the folder?"

"Aside from photographic evidence that Hickman is innocent of the warehouse killing? Financial records that implicate him in a broad range of other criminal activities. Some of it relates to stuff even my officers hadn't found. His reach is bigger than I knew." Smithy's gaze narrowed on the sheaf of papers in his gloved hands—proper disposable gloves, not what Jack has resorted to last night. "I wonder . . ."

Graham finished his coffee and rose to refill his mug. A sleepless night on top of discovering a murder victim had left him feeling hung over, with a sick stomach and pounding head minus the throwing up. "Do you have any idea if someone is trying to set me up, and if so, why?"

"I'll let you know when I figure it out. Tell me more about the body you found. Every detail."

Recounting finding the body was different with Smithy. Incisive questions sharpened Graham's recall of small things he hadn't consciously noticed, but which Smithy explored in minute detail. Unlike Marion Brooks, Smithy didn't blanch at his description of blood spatter and asked for his professional opinion on the depth and angle of the fatal knife wound.

Maybe in trying to spare the constable's feelings he'd failed to give her essential details.

"Definitely overhand. He had to have been on the ground

when he was stabbed.”

“It doesn't sound like a typical gangland murder, especially when you look at these photos. This is more like what I would have expected if any of Hickman's gang were involved.”

Jack leaned forward and, careful not to touch the photo, tapped the table above the second image, the one showing a murderer. “Photos can be doctored of course, but didn't you say a few of Hickman's gang escaped, including his lieutenant?”

“Yes. This is a tangle of threads, but I think the Hickman case is far from over. I'm off to talk with your police sergeant. Edwards, isn't it?”

Graham sat back in his chair. “Yeah. He won't be thrilled to see you, unless you're bringing me in in handcuffs.”

“Want to try it and loosen his tongue?”

“God forbid.” Handcuffs, bars, a windowless cell—yes, he knew what the Lark Creek jail cell would be like.

*Hell on earth.*

Smithy replaced the photos and documents in the folder and restored the bundle to the way they'd found it. “When I get back, I want to see the murder scene, and the surveyor's markers.”

“Come and find me at my campsite. Jack can point you in the right direction.”

Forgetting she had a guest, Janice wandered into the kitchen. Malcolm was standing, hands resting either side of the electric kettle, his head bowed. Her best china mug sat ready, a teabag tag hanging over the rim.

"Good morning, Malcolm."

He jumped, sending the mug flying. It shattered on the tiled floor. "Christ, are you trying to scare me to death?"

"All I said was good morning. What on earth's the matter with you?" Her favourite china mug lay in pieces and her tone was as sharp as its shattered edges. She took the broom and dustpan from the cupboard and set to cleaning up the mess.

"Sorry, I'm sorry." He ran a hand through his short hair. It stood up like a bantam rooster's. "I slept badly."

"And that was without all the noise of the pub to keep you awake."

What was wrong with her? Tart comments just popped out the more she saw of Malcolm. Granted, he'd given her a dose of doubt yesterday, but even if—*no 'if' about it*, she told herself. She *was* also at fault for the death of their marriage. But she didn't want him in her face first thing in the morning.

Why was he so jumpy?

She swept up the shards of china and rose with the dustpan and brush in hand and met his gaze. "I think it would be best if you went back to the hotel, Malcolm. Unless of course you're heading back to Brisbane today?"

"I can't do that. I can't go." The words fell around her like hailstones, rapid, loud, and threatening to her peace of mind. She hated hailstorms. Hated confrontation and being put on the spot. Hated the sense of being used.

"I know you can. Pack your gear, get in your car, and drive. It's that easy."

"And what about us trying again? I love you, Janey."

"We both know it's not going to happen. I admit you gave me plenty to think about yesterday, and I apologised for the hurt I unwittingly caused you. But I've moved on. There isn't another life together for us. It's over. It's been over since you walked out."

Before her eyes Malcolm's pleading expression—the look that sat so alien on his face—dropped away, replaced by a cold sneer.

"Let me put it this way so your puny brain can't mistake what I'm telling you. I am going to stay here with you, in our rediscovered marital bliss.

What the hell was happening here? Was he having some kind of episode?

"You're not."

"I am. You can accept it or I can tie you up in your bedroom. Your choice, but I'm not going anywhere. Not until I get the money."

Fear flickered through Janice, slithering like a snake through her disbelief. Her gaze darted to the door into the laundry. Closed, and he'd catch her before she got to the back door. In her hands she held a dustpan full of china shards.

Anything could be used as a weapon.

She'd read that somewhere. Could she throw the contents into his face? Was he close enough for her aim to be true?

Running her tongue over her dry lips, she eyed off the distance.

*Keep him talking, get a little closer first.*

"What money, Malcolm?"

"Your inheritance. Don't tell me your grandmother's lawyers haven't been in touch?"

"I have no idea what you're talking about." The idea was absurd. "Any inheritance would go to my father, not me."

"A letter came for you, redirected to my address."

"And you opened it?" She edged a little closer. Another step and she'd have a chance of hitting him in the face with the pieces of china.

"Naturally, when I saw the solicitor's name on the envelope. Their letter seemed like the answer to all my problems."

"You have money problems?" She reached the edge of the table, her chosen point of attack.

"Of course. You were always a bit dim, Janey, but I knew you'd have your uses. I hoped it would be to give me an heir so I would become my father's choice to take over the family company, but you even failed at that."

Fury guided Janice's aim. She flung the contents of the dustpan at Malcolm, turned and fled through the front door.

## Chapter 18

Graham had tidied his campsite and taken stock of his supplies while he waited for Smithy's return. The pot of honey he'd retrieved from his supply of dry goods to make the cake for Janice sat on top of a storage cube. He wouldn't be visiting her until this was all over.

He could borrow Jack's phone and text her. And he'd have to find a way to keep Rick off the ridge.

Neither would be easy; both would be better done from a distance, but a text message wouldn't cut it with his son.

"Graham?" Smithy was making no effort to be quiet. Even in his distracted state Graham heard the Federal police officer's approach.

"You're on the right track. Keep coming." Lifting the coffee pot off the fire, he poured two mugs and handed one to Smithy before he could sit on the log Graham had drawn up in front of the fire. "No chair, sorry. It fell apart during the police search."

"Bit rough, were they?"

"Yeah. Do you want to have your coffee first?"

"I'll bring it with me. I passed a surveyor's marker on my way here. Let's go back and start there."

In the golden light of late afternoon, Graham led Smithy from marker to marker. Smithy set his mug on the ground and pulled a map of the area from his pocket. "So we've got markers here, here, and here."

"The others are—" Graham took the map and set a finger on the positions of the remaining markers. "That's all of them."

Smithy noted the positions and then held the map at arm's length and looked from it to the view beyond. "Does anything strike you about the area covered by this survey?"

"It's everything not owned by the Donovan family between here and Cottage Farm, including the area where my beehives are and all the plants I've established over the years."

"Right, but above this line the ground becomes rocky, too stony for growing much."

"Makes sense you'd want better land for house blocks I suppose."

"Look at the distance from Jack's place to each of the markers again."

Graham checked the scale at the bottom of the map and suddenly, he saw what Smithy had already noticed. "None of the markers is more than a kilometre from the cottage. I see that, but what does it mean?"

"I don't know yet. Come on, show me where the murder happened while we've got the light."

"Do you want the approach from my camp, or the easy way

along the bank of the creek?"

Smithy pounced on the question like a cat on a chase toy, both his gaze and understanding sharp. "The murderer used your knife. I assume it was at your campsite?"

"In its sheath on top of my cupboard. In plain sight if anyone was looking."

"Then we'll start there and make our way down to the hives. How did your bees take the intrusion?"

"Not well. Are you an apiarist too?" Although Graham knew there was a beekeeping group that met in Dalton, most of what he knew had been gleaned from books. That was the problem with—his problems. And not having a vehicle. "It would be great to chat to a fellow apiarist."

Except for the fact he knew his way around both his campsite and most of the ridge even in the dark, he would have stumbled. That odd wisp of thought—*of desire to* talk *to other people*—blindsided him.

Smithy's remark barely skimmed the surface of his consciousness. "No. They interest me though. Nature's most important workers, in my book. Show me the way you think our man went."

"I know which way he went. Left a trail a blind man could see." Pointing out a freshly scraped branch here, a crushed plant there, Graham led the way to the creek, stepping carefully around the signs of the murderer's passage.

"How do you know it was the murderer who came this way and not a random walker or police officer?" Smithy followed Graham, sometimes stepping in his footsteps and at others, taking a parallel path to the perp's.

"His gait. He rolls his right foot when he walks." Crouching beside an intact footprint, Graham pointed at the outside ridge. "See how he leaves a deeper ridge on this side? It's consistent with footprints I found in the ash of my campfire, before the boys in blue obliterated the signs. I picked up his trail after the police finished their search. The footprints match a partial right footprint beside where the body was found."

Smithy pulled out his phone and a builder's tape measure, which he opened and set alongside the footprint and took photos of both. "I see the signs when you point them out. What did the police say when you showed them?"

"They didn't see any of it. They didn't ask my opinion; just wanted to know the easiest way to reach the creek hives. I showed them the easy route. And yes, that was before I found his tracks."

"And I am certain you intended to let them know this detail at your earliest convenience. Lucky for me I just happened to be the first official you saw after you found them." Smithy's gaze seemed without guile, but Graham got the message.

"Lucky for me you turned up."

"And you preserved the small signs of our perp." Smithy stood, put his tape measure into his pocket and nodded. "I knew there was a reason I liked you."

"Enough to recommend me for more work in witness protection?"

This time Smithy's all-seeing blue gaze narrowed. "Ready to make a sea change? I never thought you'd leave your mountain."

Graham shrugged. "A man just needs a good enough reason. Not sure about leaving the mountain permanently though. Here it is."

Police tape fluttered in a light breeze and the chill in the air promised a cold night as they reached the second set of hives. Smithy walked carefully around the perimeter of Graham's second apiary. It pained Graham to leave the damaged hive broken, but antagonising Edwards by retrieving and repairing it was a bad idea. Besides, the dispossessed bees had gone.

Had they joined the other hives?

"The body was here, head towards the creek. You can see the blood spatter on the hive."

"Did the police open any of the hives?"

"Only the one that was knocked over. All they got for their trouble was sticky fingers and stings." Grim humour seemed all he could offer as he looked at the fallen hive. Losing the hive was like losing part of his family.

Smithy nodded. "I get why they looked in the hive, but I think we'll have more luck tracking down whoever paid for that survey to be done."

"Jack got a name—Fiesta Holdings. Private company."

"Then that's where I'll get the team to start looking. Now tell me, have you pissed off anyone lately?"

Janice heard Malcolm crashing around her kitchen, yelling and screaming before the front door banged shut behind her, muffling the sounds.

Where could she go before he could see well enough to follow?

Broad daylight and open paddocks limited her options.

Unless she could reach the crest in the road and drop down into a ditch.

Would that be enough shelter?

If he was in his car. But what if he came after her on foot?

Holding her dressing gown clear of her legs, she ran. Her slippers slapped on the bitumen strip. Chest pounding, she ran towards the rise in the road.

*Nearly there, nearly . . .*

His angry roar tore through the air. "I'll get you, you bitch."

Too late to hide. All she could do was run like the wind and hope she'd limited his vision with the broken china and that he lost sight of her on the other side of the rise.

Puff. Pant. Gasp. Groan.

She pressed a hand against the stitch in her side and kept running, bending and putting pressure on her aching, not-young-enough-for-this-sudden-exertion-without-stretching body.

Lantana grew along one side of the road forming an impenetrable barrier for fifty metres. A few scrubby trees grew along the other side. All she needed was a fallen branch, a stone—no, she'd have to be too close to use it. Her aim had always been lousy.

Would Malcolm kill her if he caught her?

She didn't know. Even in their darkest days, when his emotional abuse had peaked, she'd never thought him capable of *that*.

Emotional abuse—finally she could name it for what it was. *Was that when I stopped loving him?*

This new version of her husband frightened her. Shocked and appalled her.

Her heart thumped hard. Between the blood rushing in her ears and her gasping breaths she couldn't hear Malcolm's approach and she didn't dare turn to look. Charging over the rise, looking for anything to protect herself with, her desperate gaze flicked up to the ridge.

*Please be looking down from your mountain, Graham. I need you.*

Casting her fate to chance she did a mental coin toss, jumped the ditch and headed into the trees. Not far beyond, several termite mounds had grown up. Hard as concrete, they offered scant shelter, but the ground had dips and hollows. She ducked behind the furthest mound. Her breathing sounded loud, harsh, panicky. She *was* panicking.

*Calm down and think.*

Her nearest neighbour's house was still a good three hundred metres distant. Too far to outrun Malcolm.

"Janey, come out and I won't hurt you."

Sickly-sweet, pseudo-friendly.

She hated his voice. Hated the abomination of what he'd become. Hated the pet name she'd once thought cute.

How had he caught up with her so quickly? Had her aim been so bad he'd only caught the dust in his eyes?

Making herself as small as possible she pressed closer to the termite mound.

*Too late to run.*

Fear snatched the air from her lungs. She couldn't breathe. Her chest hurt, her lungs hurt, and she was more afraid than she'd ever been.

Where was he?

Slowly she leaned sideways, peering over her shoulder and around the mound.

Malcolm stalked through the long, dry grass between the trees. Towards the mounds. Blood ran down one side of his face.

*I hurt him, but not enough to stop him.*

She had seconds to come up with something. Seconds . . .

She peeped around the mound again.

If she made a break for the fence, maybe she could get close enough to scream for help. Eyeing the distance to the bottom boundary of her neighbour's property, movement outside the distant farmhouse caught her attention. Young Sophie was pushing her little brother on the swing Neil had set up for his children.

One quick peep around the mound to check—no Malcolm. Had he given up on the paddock and returned to the road?

She launched herself towards the fence as fast and as quietly as she could.

Twenty metres.

Ten metres . . . five.

She tripped—crashed to the ground.

Malcolm's arms were around her knees. The pressure eased.

A brief respite.

She tried to push herself up.

"No, you don't." Malcolm's weight covered her body, crushed her, pushed her face-first into the dirt. "We're going to have a chat about how well we're getting on now we've reconnected. And if you try another little stunt like that last one, I'm going to hurt you—bad."

Susanne Bellamy

**Chapter 19**

". . . so I'm doing the training to become involved in witness protection." Graham sat back in the squatter's chair and drank the beer Rick had poured for him.

"That's great, Dad, although I thought you were going to talk to Janice about setting up some sort of outdoor activity centre for kids like Kaden. What happened to that?"

"Janice did look into what was involved for me. In the end I decided the red tape would kill me. A man could drown in red tape and no one would notice until the stink got to them."

Rick chuckled. "Ah, yes, bureaucracy at its finest. Make things so damned hard that people give up and go away and the status quo remains. I reckon that's where red tape came from, coloured by the blood, sweat and tears of people trying to change the system."

"Yep. Anyway, son, I won't be around for a little while."

"Do you want me to pop up and check the hives for you?"

"No, I won't be gone that long, but I don't want you chasing up the ridge and worrying that you can't find me. Speaking of which, can I borrow your phone? I need to let Janice know."

"How's that going, getting to know Janice?" Rick thumbed his phone open and handed it to Graham.

"We're just friends, Rick. That's all. Her ex-husband is

back in town, trying to win her back I reckon."

Except the truth was more complicated than this.

The time he'd spent with Janice had changed him, and changed what he wanted.

He liked her. She was a woman he could imagine coming home to, and now, he wanted a chance to see if that might be possible.

"And you're just going to sit back and let him? That's not the father I know."

"She's old enough to make up her own mind. Give a woman space and a chance to decide for herself; she'll make the best choice for her."

"What if she doesn't choose you?"

His gut ached with the possibility. A very real possibility by any standard, but he was no quitter.

"It's her choice. That's what's most important."

"And what about what you want? You like her, I know you do. You need to fight for her, not back off, especially not now her ex is in town. He left her and now he comes crawling back and you're not willing to stick around . . ."

"She'll understand this is work. I respect her—too much to push. Now," he held up the phone and waggled it, "do you mind if I make my call?"

Rick didn't look happy with Graham, but he retreated to the other end of the veranda, giving the illusion of privacy. Not that

Rick would try to eavesdrop, but he'd made it clear he wasn't happy with Graham's decision.

Under other circumstances—like not being a *person of interest* in a murder investigation—Graham would have been at Janice's now. Something had shifted in his life with the discovery that Rick was his son, and he wanted to pursue that change. Find out if he could reconnect with the world. With life.

He had to think he had a chance.

With Janice. When this was all over, he would ask her.

But until he knew if he was a target he wasn't going near anyone after tonight.

Janice's phone rang and rang. Finally her voice mail message began and ended before Graham had worked out what to say. He'd psyched himself up to speak to her, expecting her to engage in the social pleasantries until he found the words. But that beep at the end of her invitation to leave a message threw him. "It's Graham—Peyton. Um, I'll try calling later. It's about dinner." He pressed the end call button.

His finger hovered over the button. Should he call her back knowing that he'd have to leave a message?

He wanted to hear her voice for real, hear her reaction. He wanted to know if she was disappointed he wouldn't be there.

"Wasn't she picking up?" Rick strolled along the veranda and leaned against the railing facing Graham.

Graham handed Rick's phone back. "No, and I left an

incomplete message. I forgot to say I won't be able to make dinner at her place."

"She invited you to dinner? You, not her ex, and you still won't go?"

"It's a thank you dinner, nothing more than that."

"Just the two of you. No ex included?"

"Enough, Rick."

Janice tugged against the rope tying her hands together and tethering her to the leg of the bed end.

Tugged. Twisted. Cursed.

To no avail. All she'd achieved was raw patches around her wrists and a trickle of blood. The sight and smell made her sick. She sucked in a breath and tried to calm the roiling in her stomach. Perhaps what made her sick was the uncertainty of her situation.

Malcolm had gone mad and mad people were unpredictable.

She'd heard him on the phone to her school office earlier, heard lies fall so glibly from his mouth. "No, Janice isn't well so I'm staying with her to look after her . . . That's right, I'm her husband, well, yes, we were divorced, but now we're back together . . . That's right, living in her house. So very happy, yes, thanks, I'll tell her."

There wouldn't be a single person in Lark Creek who wouldn't accept Malcolm's story as gospel. Most knew she'd been depressed; a couple of good friends knew how deep that depression had cut and would be happy that things had worked out in the end.

No one knew the truth. No one knew that she was over her lovesick grief, or that she had given Malcolm his marching orders.

*So much for sticking up for myself. I'd be better off if I hadn't chosen this morning to speak up. I wish Graham were here. Graham!*

He knew she hadn't been thrilled with Malcolm's return. She'd told him so short a time ago that their Saturday dinner would be just the two of them. No Malcolm, and Graham had seemed pleased at that.

Would he believe she'd had such an about face as Malcolm was spreading through town?

Maybe, but she'd take any hope, even the slim chance that Graham would at least call her if he got wind of Malcolm's misinformation. And when he called, she'd find a way to communicate her predicament.

"I'll check in with Jack once a week then." Graham offered his hand.

Smithy shook it. "He's happy to be your contact. If you're serious about taking on witness protection duties, I can expedite the paperwork. Shouldn't be an issue after the way you looked after Kaden."

"Thanks."

"I'll square your disappearance with Edwards too, don't worry. He won't come looking for you." Smithy nodded and then slipped away; his departure much quieter than his arrival. Was that a sign of the seriousness of the situation?

The hiding spot he'd chosen was high and easily defended; almost impossible to find if a person didn't know it existed. While it would make moving about in daylight risky, he would have a wide view of both near and far terrain.

Stowing supplies in the backpack, he ran through preparations first made long ago; back in the early days when enemy raids were fresh in his memory and being prepared was the difference between living and dying. He'd kept the rations in the cave fresh, using each trip to the heights of the ridge as a training exercise when he changed over the supplies. Sufficient water for drinking, but not bathing. That, he could do at night in the creek when he could no longer stand the smell of himself.

He dropped the flaps of his tent and secured the upper and middle ties. Jacky could still get in and out of the loose bottom flaps. He looked around. The chicken was off in the bush somewhere. She would be fine with what she foraged, and the water in the old dog bowl would last until his next nocturnal visit to the camp.

He looked around his campsite. Already it had a deserted air about it. Grimly, Graham set off towards the ridge, taking a circuitous route . . . just in case anyone had him in their sights.

He'd make the final climb after sunset, just as he had with Anna and Kaden.

"Out of sight, out of mind, old man." Rick's teenage comment flitted through his mind. He'd merely been observing that most people in town wouldn't spare Graham a thought because they never saw him; didn't really know him.

But Graham knew the value of not being on anyone's radar. Living his life the way he wanted was an excellent result.

But there were times lately when he wondered if, just maybe, he'd moved past that point. He wanted Rick to think of him.

Would Janice think about him?

He hoped so, and he hoped that one day she'd forgive him for their cancelled dinner. If Graham had better social skills, he wouldn't have made a hash of leaving that message. The best he'd been able to come up with was a compromise; asking Rick to phone her for him and apologise. Rick wouldn't elaborate on his father's excuse.

Not if he believed the story about Graham moving into witness protection work.

Graham believed Smithy when he said he would make it happen.

Through the slow hours of afternoon, Graham waited patiently. He scanned the streets of Lark Creek and the lower slopes of the ridge. His binoculars strayed more often than they should to where Janice's house sat at the dead end of her street and to the silver car parked behind her ute.

Rick had asked what he would do if she didn't choose him.

Now he knew.

He would let her go.

He'd give up the dream invested in the idea of getting to know Janice better. He'd give up the idea of a different life.

She had never been his. That privilege belonged to Malcolm Lehman.

*I hope he understands how special she is this time around.*

When daylight faded to black, Graham moved out of the tree cover and began climbing. The cave was on the south-western horn of the saddle of the ridge and even more difficult to reach than the narrow passage through which he'd taken Anna and Kaden to safety.

By the time his hand found the narrow fissure in the rock face that pointed the way to the cave entrance, the pack on his back felt heavier than the weight of its contents. With him he carried his broken promise to Janice, and the half-truths he'd told Rick to keep his son safe. And on top of those, crushing him with disappointment, was the lost chance with Janice.

He thought about that lost chance inside the cave as he cooked noodles over a small gas flame. He thought about it as he lay, sleepless in his sleeping bag while stars circled overhead. He thought about it when the first rays of sunlight touched his face and he looked out over Lark Creek, down Janice's street.

The silver car was still parked behind her ute.

That was it then. She'd made her choice.

**Chapter 20**

"Good morning, Janey, my dear. I hope you slept well." Malcolm set a tray on the floor beside her.

Curled up on the floor, she'd hardly slept. Even with the heater on, the timer switch had turned it off when she would normally have been under her doona. But Malcolm had never liked hearing her complain about anything. In his current state of mind, she wasn't going to push any boundaries. "Fine, thank you, Malcolm."

Path of least resistance. Get him onside. Find a way to escape.

"That's my girl. Oh dear." He picked up her bound hands and turned them this way and that, examining the chafing, checking the knots.

Pain lanced down her arms. Not just pins and needles. Malcolm bent her wrists, abrading the raw wounds beneath the rope. She hissed, unable to control an involuntary shudder.

"You weren't trying to escape, were you? That would be silly and useless."

"I'm a restless sleeper."

"So long as that's all it is, Janey. You really don't want to make me angry again." He kissed her knuckles, looked into her eyes and then squeezed her wounded wrists. "Do you?"

Janice sucked in a breath. Even biting down on her lower lip wasn't enough distraction to stop a lone tear leaking from her eye. "No." Her voice was breathy, submissive. The tear ran down her cheek and dripped off her chin.

But it seemed to pacify Graham.

"I've made coffee and a piece of toast with honey."

"Thank you." She reached for the mug, part of her plastic picnic set, she noted. He wasn't about to trust her with anything that could do damage to him, but she kept the wry thought to herself. Her bound wrists made picking up the mug impossible. Maintaining the submissive expression, the subdued voice, she looked up at him. "Will you untie me so I can eat please?"

"Untie you?" His hand rose and touched the dressing on his cheek. "Hmm, I think not. Do the best you can, and if you can't manage it won't hurt you to go without. You could stand to lose a few kilos, Janey. You've let yourself go."

He grinned and left, closing the door with a sharp click.

Real tears fell then. Tears of anger, tears of frustration, tears of despair.

And when she'd released all of them, she leaned against the bed and stared at the narrow bands of daylight between the Venetian blinds. No one was coming to her rescue. No one knew she was a prisoner in her own home.

By now, Graham had probably seen Malcolm's car parked overnight behind hers and drawn the wrong conclusion—the only conclusion that would make sense. She doubted he would phone to cancel dinner.

In Graham's mind, Malcolm's car sitting in her driveway would negate the invitation.

Glancing at the breakfast tray, simple but tantalising with its promise of sustenance, she knew she had to find a way to eat and drink. Losing her energy was a short road to losing hope.

*I won't give Malcolm that satisfaction.*

Her wrists were bound too tightly; there was no give in the rope, as she'd found out the hard way. But if she wriggled onto her stomach, could she reach the mug? Grip the rim in her teeth and tip it enough to drink?

On her third attempt she managed to control the flow. Sure, she made a mess. A pool of spilled coffee surrounded the mug, but her parched throat felt a little less dry. She eyed off the toast. A different proposition.

Twisting her hands caused a flare of pain, like a line of fire around her wrists. Determined not to be beaten, she stretched a little further. Fingers touched a piece of toast, dug in and pulled it towards her, closed on the crust. She lifted it, angled her head so she didn't have to twist her hands again, clamped her teeth into the toast and ripped off an oversized mouthful.

Heaven on rye bread.

Sweet honey hit her tongue and she closed her eyes. The taste made her think of Graham. Honey from Graham's bees—

honey he had collected, bottled and sent down the hill—was in her home. In her hands, sustaining her.

The thought sustained her, brought Graham closer as she chewed, swallowed, repeated. By the time she'd eaten all the toast, she knew.

Come hell or high water, she would survive. She would get out of here and when she did, she was going to find Graham and convince him to—do what? Take a chance on her?

The bedroom door opened, and Malcolm entered. He appeared less than pleased when he saw the empty plate and mug. "You made a mess, Janey. You know I don't like it when you leave a mess."

Anger rose in her, swelled up and filled the hollow spaces within, but self-preservation was a powerful force too. Janice lowered her gaze.

Placate. Submit. Endure.

"I'm sorry, Malcolm. Do you mind if I use the bathroom now?" Her bladder was fit to burst, but now she'd eaten and she had a handle on Malcolm's state of mind. At least she thought she did.

His smirk confirmed it. "Much better, Janey." He untied the rope from the bed leg and, putting a hand under her elbow, helped her to stand. Pins and needles in her feet and a cramp in her hip made her stagger.

Smirk.

*He loves seeing me so weak.*

She offered her roped wrists. "I don't think I can use the toilet like this."

"We can't have you making any more messes, can we?" He smirked again but released the knot and shepherded her into the ensuite.

Blood pulsed into her hands and fingers, painful, and yet she welcomed the pain. The sense of elation over winning the small concession buoyed her and she bit down on her lower lip again. "Thank you, Malcolm."

He even let her close the door between them. "I'll wait here for you. I don't want you hurting yourself in your weakened condition. Such a shame you've had a relapse of that awful virus."

She knew precisely what he meant. Understood the threat implied.

*Try to escape and I'll hurt you and it will be your fault for defying me.*

Message received, loud and clear.

Patience, Janice. Patience, planning, and preparation.

Behind the cistern, the small, screened window might let a child through, but not a grown woman. When she made her escape attempt, she had to succeed. Failure was too awful to contemplate.

"Janey, there's a Rick Peyton on the phone demanding to speak with you."

"Rick?"

"Graham's son. I'm going to let you tell him very nicely to pass on a message to his father that you don't want to see him anymore. Okay? Can you do that for me?"

Janice blinked, her mind racing. The unexpected had happened and she hadn't worked out a message to convey her situation. She nodded and reached for her mobile.

Malcolm scrutinised her face and whipped the phone out of her reach, his hand covering the microphone. "Maybe not. You've lost the look of contrition." He backed away from her and raised the phone to his ear. "Rick? I'm sorry, but Janey is sound asleep. That virus she had is back. Any message?" He listened, grinned, and pinned Janice with a gaze that gloated. "Sure, I'll tell her when she wakes up."

He tossed her phone onto the bed. "Seems your mountain man is a coward. He got his son to phone and tell you he can't keep your dinner date after all."

A lump of regret and disappointment filled Janice's throat, but she nodded, swallowed, aimed for a conciliatory expression. "Perhaps he's heard that we're back together again."

"We are, aren't we?" Malcolm strutted to the door and back. "We are together. I need to phone the lawyer and tell him. You can tell him too and he'll release the money from his trust account."

"Yes, Malcolm. I can tell him that. What do you need the

money for?"

Crafty eyes, mad eyes, eyes that had never belonged to the husband she had known, looked down on her. "It's for my business."

"I didn't know you'd set up in business. What do you—"

"You don't need to know any of it."

"No, you're right. I'm not very good with numbers."

Was there any way to alert the lawyer to her situation? Probably not.

She didn't know her grandmother's lawyer and he didn't know her.

Annoyed and stiff from sitting for hours on end on the floor, Janice rolled onto her knees. Malcolm had changed the bloodied rope after her last bathroom visit. His fastidiousness about touching it overcame his desire to prolong her suffering and the new rope wasn't as thick, but it was longer.

*Long enough to let me lie on the bed?*

Easing the rope as high up the leg of the bed as it would go, she tested its length. If she put her arms over her head, she could lie down. Toeing off her muddy ruined slippers, she settled her hip on the edge of the bed, stretched and rolled onto her back. Even with her arms stretched up over her head, the mattress beneath her aching body felt good.

Bliss.

"Janey, see how nice I am to you. You have a comfortable bed you can lie in all day long and your husband to bring you food. Aren't you a lucky woman?"

Janice opened her eyes. *Did I go to sleep?*

Blinking and trying to gather her sleep-scattered thoughts, she realised it must be late afternoon. Dust motes danced in narrow bars of sunlight striping the air. "Very lucky, thank you, Malcolm."

"I have your grandmother's solicitor on the phone, and he wants to hear from you that we are back together."

How she wished she could sit up, look him in the eye, meet him as an equal. Did she really want to be an equal with a madman?

"Certainly."

Malcolm turned on the speakerphone function and held the phone near her mouth. "Hello?"

"Mrs Lehman? Nice to finally hear from you. Is it your wish that we deposit funds currently held in trust into your joint account?"

"That's correct. I assume there will be forms to sign?"

"Yes. I'll put them in the post. It will take a couple of weeks—"

Malcolm covered the microphone and shook his head. "No, too long."

Was that a flash of fear in his eyes?

Janice frowned. Whatever was going on with her ex,

money was at the heart of it, and if he was afraid, she'd make a guess the amount he needed was substantial.

"Is there a quicker way to sign the documents? We'd like to access the funds as soon as possible."

"I could email them to a local solicitor, and he could witness your signature? Would that be satisfactory?"

Janice looked at Malcolm.

He nodded. "Do it today," he whispered.

"That would be satisfactory. Jack Donaldson is the local lawyer. Could you do it today?"

"I'm afraid not, but I'll get my secretary onto it first thing in the morning. Make a time to see your solicitor and we'll get this sorted for you as soon as possible." The lawyer ended the call.

Malcolm traced a finger down the side of her face and touched her lips. "Well done, Janey. Sometimes even you can come up with a good idea."

Clenching her muscles, she controlled the desire to shudder and shy away from his touch.

*One more day and I'll be free of him.*

Sounds of a car turning into her driveway had both of them turning their heads to the covered window. Malcolm sprang off the bed and parted two slats, peering through the narrow slit. "Might be the Romney girl. The van has the winery name on it. Why would she be calling on you?"

Gei Romney was here?

"Probably because you told Rick Peyton that I'm sick again. They're in a relationship and Gei's mother is a friend. She'll be wanting to check up on me."

"Blasted small town nosy . . ." Malcolm strode out of the bedroom, slamming the door behind him, and a few seconds later, knocking sounded from the front door.

"Hello. Gei Romney, isn't it?"

She heard the front door close. Filtered voices reached Janice through the walls. She wriggled to the edge of the bed. Her bare foot caught on a tissue from under her pillow. She looked at the man size tissue, hanging like a white flag of surrender.

There was no chance Malcolm would let her speak with Gei, but if Janice could reach the window with her foot . . .

Scrunching her toes over the tissue, she rolled off the bed, hitting the floor with a thump. Ignoring her sore hip, she worked her legs up the wall and under the Venetian blind. Her foot should be visible above the window ledge, but would Gei have any reason to look this way?

It was a long shot, but she had to try.

She moved her leg back and forth as fast as she could, waving her white flag. Not a flag of surrender, but a flag of defiance, a flag of hope.

And she prayed as she hadn't prayed in years. Not since her prayers for a child had fallen on deaf ears.

## Chapter 21

Graham crept under cover of darkness past Jack's garden shed and slipped under the eaves of the woodshed without activating the sensor lights. Having installed the system, he knew the location of every sensor. Cupping his hands, he called the *oom, oom, oom* cry of the Mopoke owl, as agreed with Jack.

Moments later, he heard the back door open and close. No lights showed in the cottage as Jack crossed the yard and joined Graham under the woodshed roof.

"I thought you'd be down tonight. We deactivated the system."

"And here was me congratulating myself on avoiding the sensors."

"You did. Anna only turned it off after I heard your call. It sounds like a car that won't start."

"Any news?"

In the darkness, Graham was attuned to small sounds. A brief sigh slipped from Jack.

"I had a strange request late this afternoon at my office, purporting to come from Janice Lehman."

"What do you mean, purporting?"

Silence stretched between them, a silence crackling with

such tension that Graham imagined an ethical battle waging within the lawyer. If Jack's face were visible, he knew it would bear a frown.

"I'm guessing she's your client. It's okay, Jack. I know you can't divulge details."

"It was her ex-husband who rang to make an appointment for me to witness their signatures releasing Janice's inheritance into their joint bank account. And before you say anything, I do realise I'd be breaking client privilege telling you, but something about Malcolm Lehman is off, and *he* is *not* my client. And another thing—he claimed Janice is too sick to come into the office. I'm to take the documents out to her house and expedite the return of their signatures to the lawyer handling her grandmother's estate."

"Janice is sick again? That doesn't sound right. She climbed to the lookout with me. Not one hundred per cent fit yet, but nothing to indicate—"

"Lehman claimed she'd had a relapse and he's moved into the house to look after her. Also claims they're back together again."

He'd wondered about that but hearing confirmation from Jack twisted the screws. His heart, that piss-poor organ that insisted on beating despite his occasional wish to the contrary, shrivelled a little more.

He did care for Janice. Now, when it was too late, he admitted his liking for her was strong; strong enough he'd considered pursuing it further.

"Lehman's car has been parked at her place for the past couple of days. I've seen him in the yard on his phone, but no sign of Janice."

"And there's another thing. Gei phoned me not long ago. She said she dropped by Janice's home to see if there was anything she could do to help. Lehman wouldn't let her in to see Janice; reckoned she was asleep. Gei said he seemed on edge the short time she was there."

Something snapped inside Graham. "Something about this stinks. I'm going over there."

Jack grabbed his arm. "Do you think that's wise? Smithy's relying on you to keep a low profile while he does some digging. If something happens to you—"

"Jack, nobody will know I'm there, I can guarantee you."

"I'll come with you."

"No offence, but you don't have the necessary skill set for guerrilla tactics."

"I can drive you down faster than you can walk and be your back up man if the need arises."

Graham thought about arguing, but Jack was right. It would be a lot quicker by car, and if something wasn't right for Janice, a vehicle could be useful.

But he couldn't imagine what was likely to be wrong, other than the fact Janice had chosen her ex over him. The only reason he had for checking was that he disliked Lehman.

But he had to see for himself. He had to know.

"Let's go."

"I'll get the car keys and tell Anna where we're going." Jack crossed the yard to the cottage. A faint green glow blinked on and off as he opened the back door and closed it behind him.

Graham was waiting beside Jack's car by the time he reappeared.

"All set. We won't have any element of surprise though. Isn't her road a dead end?"

"Yes, but there's another way in. Do you know Dryden's Lane?"

By the light from the dashboard he saw Jack frown. "Haven't heard of it."

"It's an old track through the property at the dead end of Janice's road. We can come up to the house from the rear."

The waning moon hung low in the western sky, its light feeble but enough to make out the track ahead. Jack switched off the headlights and drove slowly, bumping over ruts and through potholes. They passed a clanking windmill and heard the soft bleating of a goat disturbed by their passage.

"It's maybe two hundred metres ahead." Graham peered through the darkness and was rewarded by the glow of a light through the amber glass of Janice's front door. "Stop here."

"Looks like someone's awake." Jack eased off the accelerator, pulled up in the cover of scrubby trees and low bushes and switched the engine off. "You sure you don't want me to come with you?"

"I'm sure."

"Want to signal if you need me?"

"You'll know if I need you, Jack. If that point comes, it will be obvious. Don't be a hero and come charging in unless you're certain. If something is wrong, I'll bring Janice back here."

"And if both Gei and I are wrong, and Janice is settled back into her comfy married life with Lehman?"

"In that case I'll be back alone."

He closed the passenger door quietly and made his way to the back of Janice's house.

There was no security system to avoid, and no dog warning of an intruder. Both should have concerned him. Janice was a woman living on her own and one or both safety measures would have made sense. But as Graham approached the rear of the house, for once, he was grateful for her choices. He was at the corner of the garden shed when the back door opened.

Graham dropped to the ground before Malcolm Lehman stepped out onto the porch, phone in hand.

A scant twenty metres separated them.

Light from Lehman's phone screen lit his face as he held it near his mouth.

Gleeful, Graham thought, although maybe it was more grimace than grin.

When Lehman spoke, Graham decided he was trying to sound upbeat. "It's me. It will be done tomorrow. The money will go into my account and as soon as it's cleared . . ."

There was a pause and Lehman's face turned a sickly pale shade.

Did Graham imagine the bobbing of the man's throat, the trembling of his hand holding the phone to his mouth?

"Of course. The message you sent was clear." The screen went dark.

Next moment the sound of Lehman throwing up carried to Graham, with a smell that confirmed it.

"Shit." Lehman sat on the concrete step, head bowed. He looked like he wasn't going to move any time soon.

The waiting chafed Graham's patience.

Lehman was after Janice's money and he'd done something to make sure he got his hands on it.

Did Janice know this, or had Lehman convinced her he was back for her alone?

Crawling backwards, Graham retreated around the back of the shed and down the side of the house. While Lehman sat outside feeling sorry for himself Graham would check on Janice.

The Venetian blinds were closed at her bedroom windows, but he'd noticed the poorly fitted blinds left a narrow gap at one end when he'd cracked the window to let in fresh air when she was sick. It felt like ancient history since he'd cared for Janice during her illness instead of only a couple of weeks.

Keeping his back to the cold brick wall, he made his way between the house and two waist-high azalea bushes. The window ledge sat at shoulder height. Slow and silent, he peered around the edge of the bricks.

A sliver of bedroom was visible in the soft light of Janice's bedside lamp. The doona hung in an untidy pile, spilling over the edge of the bed.

Janice was much tidier than that, unless . . .

Scrunching his eyes closed, Graham sucked in a breath through gritted teeth. Was rumpled bedding sufficient proof he should mind his business and leave?

Half-turned to do just that, a soft sound—part-whimper, he thought—stopped him. Lehman was around the back having puked his guts beside the back steps.

Was that sound a sign of a trouble woman?

Should he let Janice know he was here?

Trying not to second-guess himself, Graham cupped his hands. The soft *oom, oom* wouldn't travel far. He waited. Called a second time.

Would Janice remember the afternoon she climbed his hill?

Supposing she did, no reply was also an answer.

He looked one last time through the sliver.

A bare foot slid between the blinds and the windowsill. The heel barely made it past the windowsill, but the toes were painted in a soft pink nail polish and they gripped a white tissue.

It made no sense, but he knew. Janice had heard him.

"Janice?" He kept his voice low.

"Help me, Graham."

Adrenaline surged through his veins. He gripped the frame and pushed the window open. "I'm coming in." Leveraging his upper body strength, uncaring now if he alerted Malcolm, he hauled himself up and over the ledge.

The sight of Janice tied to her bed enraged him. If Lehman walked in now, he'd beat the man to a pulp.

He pulled a small knife from the holster on his calf. Smaller than the one locked in a police evidence box, but just as sharp. He cut through the rope around her wrists.

She winced and he had time to note the red welts before approaching headlights on high beam cut through the blinds. He cracked the space between two blades and peered out.

A vehicle roared over the crest of the road and turned into Janice's driveway. Big. Black. Noisy.

Four men emerged. Three were armed. Three car doors banged. The fourth man, a passenger from the back seat, stood holding his door. He made a small shooing motion towards the house.

Graham didn't wait to see more. Putting a finger to his lips, he grabbed Janice's mobile from the bedside table and drew Janice into her ensuite. Awkwardly placed above the toilet was an access point into the ceiling. *Stupid spot for a manhole,* he'd thought when he was caring for Janice. Now, he felt grateful it wasn't in the laundry as in other homes.

He gently pulled the ensuite door closed and pointed to the manhole, barely discernible in the spill of light from the front security light. Putting his mouth close to Janice's ear, he whispered, "I'll help you up. Feel for the bearers and only step on them. Okay?"

Hair brushed his cheek as she nodded.

He stood on the cistern, reached up and eased the manhole cover aside, and then turned and helped Janice onto the lid of the toilet bowl and onto the cistern. Hands at her waist, he asked, "Ready? Put your feet on my thigh. I'll lift you."

"Thank you for coming."

"Later. Now . . ." Hoisting Janice until her feet found his thigh, waiting as the soft sounds of her feeling her way filled the small bathroom, he listened to what was unfolding outside.

There had been no knock at the front door, but Lehman's startled exclamation was clear. He hadn't expected company tonight.

Janice whispered, "Give me a boost."

"Step into my hands."

Her bare foot was cold in his linked hands and he braced to

take her weight and heave her into the ceiling. Scrabbling sounds filtered down and then, "I'm in. The hole's clear."

Praying his boots weren't leaving muddy pointers to Janice's disappearance, Graham pulled himself up and settled the manhole cover in place. Careful to keep the screen of Janice's mobile pointing low, he turned it on.

His stomach spasmed.

His breath stalled.

The space beneath the low-profile roof was minimal. Uninsulated and with splinter-rough wooden beams that would cause problems for Janice, moving far from the manhole wasn't an option. Here, there was no room to stand. Barely enough room to sit up.

Bands of iron wrapped around Graham's chest.

No. Air.

Whatever had driven Graham to push her through the manhole into the roof cavity instead of through the window to freedom must be bad, but she'd follow him wherever he led. Unlike mad Malcolm, she trusted Graham.

With her life.

Reaching out a hand she touched his arm and whispered, "Thank you for rescuing me."

No reply.

She settled her hand on his arm. Bunched muscles gave her

the first clue. Ragged breathing reminded her.

*Oh my God, his claustrophobia.*

She leaned close and squeezed his arm. "Graham, I'm here. You're not alone."

Nothing. Only ragged breaths, short and sharp.

"Breathe with me, Graham. Please try to breathe with me. In, two, three, four, out, two, three, four. In . . ."

His hand closed over hers, gripped hard. His fingers brushed her injured wrist.

She sucked in a breath, tried not to flinch.

"Talk to me, Janice. Stop me thinking about where we are."

"Bend your head so I can whisper. We have to be quiet."

Hair tickled her cheek and his breath skated across her skin. Ragged breaths, choppy, panicked.

"I'm here, Graham. We're going to talk—quietly—and wait until we know what's going on. And when it's safe to do so, we'll climb down and have a cup of coffee. Okay?"

"Yes."

Letting instinct and his responses guide her, Janice talked, her lips brushing his ear, her voice, soft and steady. Nothing heavy or serious, but the flow of words, her calm voice, the connection between them—her hand on his arm and his holding her other hand—she clung to the hope that somehow, she was helping him.

After a little while his breathing seemed less ragged and she dared to ask a question. "Why did you come tonight?"

"He wouldn't let Gei see you and Jack said . . . Is Lehman blackmailing you?"

"My freedom for the money?" Hours alone and tied to her bed with nothing to do but think, her brain had wrestled with this question. "I truly don't know if he planned to let me go once he had what he wanted."

Voicing her fear was a relief. Now she was safe, relatively speaking, and a sob rose in her throat. She clamped her mouth shut. "We aren't out of the woods yet, are we?"

He released her hand.

She felt the loss of his warmth and the sense of security his touch gave her, but then he eased an arm around her shoulders and pulled her close. "It's okay, Janice. We'll get out. They don't know we're here. It's about out-waiting them. We can do it."

A shudder wracked her body. She'd been through an awful ordeal, but she was certain something worse had happened to Graham. If he could offer her comfort while battling his own fears, she could do no less.

Leaning into his warmth, her head found its way to his shoulder. She liked the feeling of her head there, his arm around her. She liked the scent of the bush that clung to his clothes. If she closed her eyes, she could imagine they were sitting in Graham's camp surrounded by native trees, the billy on the fire and Jacqueline scratching nearby.

"I think he's got big money problems. Urgent. He seemed

really afraid when Gran's lawyer said it would take a couple of weeks for the forms to arrive in the post."

"Business gone bad? What do you know?"

"Nothing."

There was a pause.

Janice squeezed his hand. He had big hands. They engulfed hers, but in a good way. "Why did you ask that?"

"I saw him on the phone before I climbed through your window. He chucked up after the call."

Random pieces dropped into place like a jigsaw taking shape . . .

Malcolm's appearance in Lark Creek as soon as he got wind of her inheritance.

The fear she'd seen in his eyes at the prospect of a delay in getting his hands on her money.

Malcolm throwing up after a call.

"He came to town to try to win me over. He needs lots of money quickly and he figured he could get all of Gran's bequest by conning me into thinking he wanted to get back together. He doesn't actually want me."

She didn't want Malcolm either, but he'd tried to use her and her insecurities and the love she'd once had for him against her.

On some deep visceral level, it still hurt.

But the new Janice gave herself a mental kick. Never again

would she let anyone use or manipulate her. Grabbing hold of her anger, she dragged it up and over the small vulnerable being who yearned for love and approval. It would always be a part of her, but her anger and refusal to yield would be her cloak. Her armour.

"From what my lawyer said after our property settlement, Malcolm has no claim against me for a share of my inheritance. He's out of time."

"Unless he got back together with you. That's the story he's putting around town. Jack told me."

"Yes. But we aren't together. I will never go back to him, to a man who abuses me and calls it love."

"That's the spirit. Jack thought there was something suss about Lehman demanding he come to the house because you were too sick to come to his office. He thought the urgency meant there might be a problem."

"And he came to you."

"I went to him. I—ah, there's stuff happening you haven't heard about yet."

"Graham, who arrived that made you head into the roof rather than out the window?"

"I don't know. But they had guns and I'm willing to guess they're the reason Malcolm puked, and why he needs the money."

## Chapter 22

Darkness and walls all around, and men with guns below. Graham wasn't comfortable or relaxed. He wasn't anywhere near feeling in control and he worried about Jack, sitting in the car and waiting for his return. And yet, with Janice snuggled up beside him—

A thin wedge of comfort split open his phobia. Sitting in the dark, his arm around Janice's shoulders, a kernel of hope took root.

A tiny sliver of control, pushing back against the darkness in his soul. He'd arrived in time to rescue her, even if they were still holed up in the . . .

*Don't think about it. Focus on how to get out in one piece.*

Janice's head rested on his shoulder. Was she asleep?

He turned his head slightly and her hair tickled his nose. What was it about her that made him feel better? For God's sake, they were sitting in the dark inside the roof and aside from one freak out, he hadn't gone stark raving mad. How was this possible?

Below them, the door into Janice's bedroom opened. Voices carried through the uninsulated ceiling, clear and loud. Words of anger and fear. Words that told Graham how precarious their position was.

"Where is she?"

"She was here, tied to the—" Lehman's was the only voice he knew.

"You said once she signed the paper, you'd have the money, so where is she?"

"Boss, the window's open." The second unknown voice sounded disinterested. It sounded like a match for the beefy fellow who'd carried the Glock.

Graham heard the rattle of blinds followed by the thud of the ensuite door hitting the wall.

"She's not in here."

Holding his breath, Graham waited.

*Not a sound. We can't make any noise or they'll hear us like we're hearing them. Did I leave any scrapes of mud from my boots?*

Their exit had been rushed. No time for finesse. No light to help their escape.

"Rope's been cut, boss."

Graham imagined the youngest man picking up the rope, holding it out for his boss's inspection.

"Lehman, let's see if I've got this right." The tone was conversational, the meaning, menacing. "You lost the money you borrowed from me and now your partner is—*gone*. Seems like you didn't understand our message and now you've lost the means to pay it back, is that right?"

"No, she was here I tell you." Lehman's voice hit the high register and ended on a gasp.

"Looks like she got out the window, boss. Want Bobby and me to scout around outside for her?"

"Go."

Sounds of footsteps leaving the room reached Graham. Two down, three still in the room. Two with guns and one rat-faced little weasel who'd sold out Janice to save his worthless hide.

"If my boys don't come back with her, you know what happens next." The boss' tone conveyed a promise.

Even with the ceiling between them Graham knew how the scene would play out. A gun dug into Lehman's back, the threat of shooting him very real.

"You know where your wife keeps the alcohol. Get me a drink." Two sets of footsteps left the bedroom, one dragging, the other steady. *Lehman and one of the men.*

Had there been a third set, or was someone still in the bedroom?

Graham thought about the threat they'd overheard. "Your business partner's gone . . . understand our message . . ."

Janice said Lehman looked sick when he saw the police poster. Was the murdered man his business partner?

Suddenly Graham wanted to get eyes on the boss. If he was the man Graham thought he might be—the man in the photos he and Jack had dug up—they needed more than Sergeant

Edwards. If it had just been him alone, he'd have considered the risk of checking acceptable, but not with Janice.

*I need to message Jack.*

As he lifted his arm from Janice's shoulders, she stirred and murmured something indecipherable.

If he could hear the men below so clearly, he and Janice would also be heard. He took hold of Janice's head and, finding her ear, whispered, "Not a word. And don't move."

He felt her stiffen, nod.

Fearing any tell-tale sign of light filtering through the ceiling from the phone, Graham shielded the screen with his body and texted Jack.

Suspect arrivals Hickman's gang. Safe in roof. Let Smithy know.

Graham mulled over their chances. Three men in the house; two outside hunting for Janice. Without eyes outside it was too risky attempting to leave by the bedroom window.

Could Jack see the men out hunting from where he was parked?

Any moment now Jack might reply. Graham bent his head close to Janice's and whispered, "Is this thing set to silent?"

"I can't remember. Give it to me." Her fingers slid along his arm and took the phone out of his hand.

Soft breaths skated across his arm and suddenly the screen lit up with Jack's silent response. Graham took the phone and read the message.

Stay put. Two outside with torches. Calling Smithy now. Then local police.

"We won't be in here much longer. Jack's calling—"

*Bang!*

Janice squeaked and slapped a hand over her mouth. By the light from the phone screen, Graham saw her wide eyes. He clicked the phone off.

*Bang!*

Janice gave a muffled yelp.

Light streamed through a bullet hole in the ceiling of Janice's bedroom.

*What the hell are they shooting at?*

Running footsteps came down the hall. "Boss? What were you shooting—"

"Spider. Hate the damned things. Have you found the drinks?"

"Yeah, some brandy and a bottle of gin that looks like it's homemade. I tasted it and it's pretty good."

*This might be my chance to get a look at him.*

Graham eased around Janice, placing his hands and feet carefully on the wooden beams. The last thing he wanted was to crash through the ceiling and land at the feet of these criminals. Setting his eye as close to the bullet hole as he could, he tried to peer into the room.

Plaster and splintered chipboard and a grey fuzz that was probably clothing, but no clear faces.

Graham moved back to sit beside Janice. With that hole in the ceiling he didn't want to risk using the phone again. He reached for her and followed her arm down to her hands. They were clamped around her calf and when he prised one off to hold and reassure her, it came away wet.

His nostrils flared at the familiar tang of metal.

The smell of blood.

**Chapter 23**

*I've been shot.*

Janice held onto her calf and gritted her teeth. The wound stung like blazes, but if she made a sound—other than that yelp—the men with guns might put more holes into both her and Graham.

Or they would keep her alive until her signature was on that document. After that, she'd be a liability.

Graham reached for her hand and she knew the moment he realised she'd been injured. His harsh inhalation cut through the fog around her brain and pain registered sharper and more focused than before.

He turned on the phone and gave it to her, aiming the light at her calf. "Hold this." Holding her ankle, he turned her leg a little. Gentle as he was, his fingers felt like instruments of torture.

She bit down on her lip.

"Superficial, thank God. Do you have a handkerchief?"

She shook her head. "I use tissues. What about the frill on my nightie?" Trembling fingers parted the lower half of her dressing gown.

Had Graham been shot during his war? Just a superficial wound made her leg feel like it was on fire.

Graham didn't hesitate. He took hold of the deep frill of her brushed cotton nightie, ripped it off and bound her calf. "We're going to get out of here now. You need to see a doctor and we need to put a stop to this mob once and for all."

"But Jack said . . . What about the men outside?"

"I'll get him to create a diversion."

Janice allowed herself to zone out while Graham texted Jack. Closing her eyes, her head tipped onto his shoulder and she inhaled the scent of bush, fresh sweat and Graham, certain she could pick him out by that alone.

"Right. Jack will text when he's in position and then we'll go back down through the manhole and out of your window."

She nodded. "Where will we go then?" Praying it wasn't far she tried to focus on the fact that soon, they'd be out of here and safe.

"Janice?" He said no more but took her hands in his.

She wished she could see his face. That single word didn't sound like Graham. There was no confidence and a whole pile of negativity behind it. The silence and not being able to read his expression weighed on her more than words.

Malcolm had used words as weapons against her. She acknowledged now what she'd refused to see during her marriage. Living with an abusive partner must be like that for other women.

*I was afraid of losing Malcolm's love and I let myself become a doormat. Never again.*

"What's on your mind, Graham?"

She heard his slow release of breath. "I'm sorry."

The phone screen lit up. *Ready.*

The single word galvanised Graham into action. He dropped one hand, slipped her phone into his shirt pocket and guided her to the manhole cover. Not a sound was made during its removal, and then he manoeuvred her into the opening. Light spilled into the ensuite from the bedroom through the open door.

She glanced at Graham.

"It's fine. Jack will be knocking at the door any minute."

As if on cue, three loud knocks sounded from the front door.

"That's him. Down you go and get to the window as quick as you can."

He grasped her arms and lowered her onto the cistern, reversing their earlier ascent. As her legs took her weight pain lanced up her injured calf like an errant ember landing on her leg when she was a child. Gritting her teeth, she took some of her weight on her arms and scrambled off the toilet lid and out of Graham's way.

Her gaze darted between his descending body and the open door. She edged along the wall and peeped around the doorjamb and then looked at Graham and nodded.

He slipped past her, took her hand and led her to the window.

From the loungeroom, Jack's voice was clear. "You

seemed in a hurry, so I thought I'd drop by tonight and get you to sign this client agreement."

"Why couldn't you bring it with the documents tomorrow. It's late." Peevish tones from Malcolm.

"I thought you'd appreciate me expediting your business. It sounded urgent."

One of the unknown voices chimed in. "Where's your car? Didn't hear it arrive?"

"Not that it's any business of yours, but a friend dropped me off while he's visiting just down the road. I walked the last bit."

Graham scooped Janice into his arms, poked his head through the window and then lifted her through the opening. The metal tracks dug into her bottom and then he lowered her until her feet touched cold dirt. She tugged her hands out of his and hopped to one side, making room for Graham. He jumped, landing lightly for a big man.

He stood in front of her, his body a shield for hers, and scanned the area. "Time to go. Climb on my back." This time he turned and squatted, reaching for her legs.

The urgency of his tone left no room for doubt. She leaned forwards and put both arms around his neck.

Arms hooked under her bottom, he rose, settled her weight and then jogged in the opposite direction she'd expected him to take.

Why was he heading away from help?

Strange as his direction seemed, she trusted him to know what was best.

Maybe if she'd done the unexpected Malcolm wouldn't have caught her.

Breathing heavily, Graham fast-jogged across the paddock, half-expecting a bullet and praying it wouldn't come. Not with Janice on his back. Any shot fired in the dark at them was more likely to hit her than him. The reality set his gut churning, but he could run faster with her on his back than in his arms.

They reached the shelter of the trees on Dryden's Lane without encountering either of the searchers. All was quiet, but he hadn't seen any stabbing beams of torchlight across the paddocks.

Graham stopped in the deepest shadows and scanned the area. He had no idea how Jack had managed to draw the searchers to the house, but he was glad the lawyer had insisted on coming with him.

*He was right. It's good to have someone who has my back.*

Janice's grip around his neck tightened as she leaned close to his ear. "You can put me down now. I must be getting heavy."

As soon as she spoke the word, his neck muscles felt the pull and his legs had a tremor they wouldn't have had five years earlier.

They'd got out alive. And while his fitness wasn't what it

should be they were free and that was all that mattered.

"I'll find Jack's car first."

Cautiously he walked in a shallow half-circle towards the car, coming at it from the rear. He paused behind a clump of wattle bushes and scanned the area ahead. Only the usual sounds of the night surrounded them.

He stepped out.

Torchlight suddenly blinded him. He set Janice down and remained between her and the man holding the torch. "Is this your car? Who are you?"

He held out a hand trying to block off the worst of the light. Behind him, Janice had grabbed hold of his jacket, but she kept quiet. "Just out with the missus."

The vague shape behind the torch matched the youngest of the men who'd arrived at Janice's.

Fit, young, and carrying a Browning GP Hi-Power.

Thirteen to fifteen shots. Standard military issue.

At ten metres, lethal.

The gunman flicked the torch over Graham's shoulder and back into his face. "At your age? You expect me to believe that?" Snide tones confirmed this was the right way to play it.

"Just trying to keep the magic alive, son. Do you mind putting that torch down? It's blinding."

The torch remained firmly in his face. "What are you doing here?"

"Is this your property? Look, sorry mate. We just wanted somewhere private you know. Didn't realise we were trespassing."

"Show me you have the keys to the car."

The subtle but unmistakeable snick of the safety being flicked reached Graham. "I left them in the car. Didn't want to lose them when we . . . You know what I mean."

"Come towards me—slowly."

"Why? Look, mate—"

"Don't you *look, mate,* me. I've got a gun. Do as I say, or you'll be sorry."

The light retreated. Graham stepped towards it, and the man with the gun. As he passed the rear of the vehicle he reached behind and applied gentle pressure to Janice's hip, pushing her away from him and towards the only possible shelter behind the vehicle.

"Open the door and show me this is your car by showing me the keys. Otherwise . . ."

Unarmed, it had been a long time since he'd faced a man with a gun. His mind knew what to do but did his body still have the speed?

Graham lifted a hand, careful to keep his movements slow. He cracked the door. *The keys are in the ignition, thanks, Jack.*

"Do you want me to take them out or do you just want to see they're where I said they were?"

The gunman came closer.

Graham waited. Waited until the younger man's gaze and torch turned to the keys.

Graham stepped to the side, grabbed the gun with one hand, twisted and slammed his other hand against the man's wrist. It jerked the gunman's arm up and Graham rammed an elbow into the man's windpipe. He went down in a choking heap and Graham held the gun.

"Darling, look in the boot and see if I left the rope in there."

Janice struggled to believe what she'd seen. The speed of Graham's move had been a blur to her; the action, like something out of a James Bond movie. But there was Graham now in possession of the gun and the man who had pulled it on them was on the ground making terrible gagging noises.

And Graham just called her darling.

Both events stunned her.

"Can you see it?"

Rope. He needed rope and she needed to help, not stand there wondering why.

"I'm looking now." She felt around for the release button and opened the boot. Jack kept a tidy toolbox, including a neatly coiled length of rope. She grabbed it and untied the slipknot with fingers that weren't quite steady. As the knot came undone, she held out the coil to Graham. "Here."

He handed her the gun and took the rope. "Keep that pointed at his chest."

Mouth dry, she held the weapon in one hand. Wondered how anyone could point it at a living being. She'd never held a gun. Dad had taught Danny to shoot with a rifle, but he hadn't believed in giving a gun to the women in his family.

In the light from the fallen torch, the tip of the gun wavered, her aim following where her gaze fell.

*Good Lord, I might hit Graham!*

She brought both hands together.

*Isn't this what they do in the movies?* The weight dragged on her injured wrists, but she was able to control it and cover the man who had threatened them with the weapon. Leaning her bottom against the car helped steady her aim. She eased the weight off her injured leg and waited while Graham tied the gunman's wrists behind his back and then tied his wrists to his ankles. The final touch was using duct tape—also found in Jack's toolbox—to gag him.

She felt no sympathy for the gunman.

Her injured wrists ached and her emotional energy was all but gone when Graham stood and took the gun from her.

He bent down and picked up the torch and gave that to her. "Are you okay?"

"Yes." But what she really wanted was to fling herself into

his arms, breathe him in and never let him go. The thought rattled her. It didn't sit well with the newly independent Janice Lehman she'd discovered she was.

Graham opened the front passenger door and offered her a hand.

As she pushed off the ground, pain like a wasp sting flared in her injured calf. She gasped.

"I'll check your wound next."

Settling into the seat, she looked at her house. "What's our next move? Are we going to leave him tied up out here and get the hell out of Dodge?"

Graham chuckled. "Sounds like you watched re-runs of Westerns when you were a kid."

"Danny loved them and I loved my big brother. I'd have sat through a horror movie if it meant I got to spend more time with him." Secretly she'd cast Danny as the gunslinger hero.

"I probably fed his confidence with my hero worship. I miss him, wherever he is."

Graham squeezed her shoulder. For a man who lived alone, he seemed to understand that she was still hurting. Still missing her brother.

"We wait here until Jack comes out. Or the police arrive; whichever happens first."

## Chapter 24

As Janice watched, Jack left her house. Malcolm stood at the front door, his gaze following as Jack walked down the driveway and turned right.

*Away from us and his car.*

"Why isn't he joining us?" Janice was struggling to keep her eyes open in the relative safety of Jack's vehicle. The sooner Jack returned, the sooner she could give in to her need to fall into a deep, deep sleep. Somewhere safe, somewhere far away from Malcolm and his ropes and his snide comments and his nasty criminal friends.

"While we were making our escape through the window, he told them he'd been dropped off. He's just keeping up the pretence of walking to a friend's place for his ride home." Graham pointed out that Malcolm only went inside and closed the door after Jack was half a paddock-length down the road. After that there was no further activity to be seen.

Janice let her head fall back onto the headrest.

She didn't care there was a man tied up outside the car. She didn't care there were men with guns in her house. Graham was here and she felt safe.

Vaguely aware of Graham rummaging for something on the

back seat, she opened her eyes and glanced sideways. It surprised her how much she could see by faint starlight and a paper-thin sliver of moon.

"I know Jack put bottles of water and food back here. Ah, got the water."

He lifted a shrink-wrapped six-pack onto his lap, opened a bottle and offered it to her. "Regardless of what happens tonight, you do understand that Malcolm is involved with these criminals and will go to jail?"

"I know. I can't imagine how or why he came to be, but there'd better be a jail term for his part in holding me hostage."

"Can't see how there wouldn't be. No man worth the name would do what he did to you, the nasty piece of—" Graham stopped short of finishing what he thought. He tipped half a bottle of water down his throat and said no more.

Janice appreciated his restraint. She felt raw and 'a bit fragile', as her mother would say. And she had a mess of emotions to sort through. Messy emotions and half a lifetime to reconsider.

*How could I have known so little about the man I married?*

Thinking about her ex-husband standing on the veranda of her home as though he owned it, she listened to Graham with half an ear and tried to decide how she felt about Malcolm.

Anger of course, but there was more than that.

She used to think he knew it all; that he was in control of his life, but he wasn't. He was weak and he'd made her feel powerless. Thankful he'd left when he did, she was also grateful for the lessons she'd learned since.

She sipped her water. At the crest of the road she could just make out Jack's figure before he slipped out of sight and shooting range. With Jack safe, the burst of adrenaline she'd been riding during their escape ebbed away. Fatigue crashed over her; waves of worry and fear—and downright terror when she thought she'd never get out of her home alive—washed away by Graham's daring rescue.

"Can we leave when Jack gets here?"

"No. I'll keep watch until Jack's friend, Smithy, gets here. You know the Federal agent I told you about?"

"I remember." But she was too tired to care. Her eyes kept closing.

"Anyway, it will take Jack a while to work his way across the paddocks and back to the car." Graham turned to her, little more than a shadowy figure in the driver's seat. "Now Jack's safe and on his way here I need to treat your wrists and check your bullet wound. Where's the torch?"

"Here." She handed the torch to him and thought about the effort required to get out of the car into the cold night air. Her bare feet had just begun to warm, tucked up under her dressing gown.

"I'm fine, Graham. Jack's message said there were two men searching for us. I don't think we should risk giving ourselves away by turning on a light."

"Open wounds need attention sooner rather than later. I'll keep the light low and behind the cover of the car." He opened his door and got out.

Offering up a quiet sigh, Janice followed him. The ground was cold underfoot, and her feet found every prickle and twig as she edged between Jack's car and a lantana bush that caught her sleeve. She pulled her arm free and hissed as her foot found a sharp stone.

She tried to be patient, tried to hold onto her gratitude and push back against the need to sleep while Graham looked through the first aid kit. He patted a spot on the tailgate. "Sit there and show me."

"Now you're being bossy." *Her tone was snippy.* Knowing fatigue and fear were the reason for her response, she tried to gather a semblance of polite apology.

Graham said nothing. In the low torchlight, he simply met her eyes and something, some ghost of emotion, passed through his.

Fearful it was pity because of what he'd probably deduced about her failed relationship with her husband, Janice sat straighter and lifted her chin.

She hated pity. No more would she be meek Janice. She was taking back the feeling of control Malcolm had stolen from her.

"You want something, you ask nicely."

Graham nodded. "You're right. Please, Janice, show me your wrists."

Extending her arms and relishing the heady sensation of freedom and power, she complied. "That's better. That sounds almost—"

Graham gently turned back the sleeves of her dressing gown.

Even in the low light, the sight of her raw wrists sent a wave of nausea ripping through her stomach.

Red. Rubbed. Raw.

Closing her eyes, she sucked in a noisy breath through her mouth.

"Tell me about Malcolm." Graham held her fingers lightly and his thumbs rubbed gently on each palm.

Her attention snapped back to Graham. She liked the feeling of him holding her hands. She'd like to have the right to hold his hands whenever she wanted.

Was she actually contemplating a relationship with him?

Trusting Graham, liking him as much as she did, there was comfort and something more in the thought. It surprised her, coming as it did hard on the heels of her hostage ordeal. A relationship meant sharing . . .

But did she want to share how weak she was; that she'd stayed in an abusive relationship for so long?

Would he think less of her if he knew what she'd only

recently acknowledged?

"Janice?"

Any good relationship started with trust and openness. It needed each party to be willing to share—the good and the bad.

"Where do you want me to start? Back when my marriage disintegrated, or do you mean start with when he showed up again on my doorstep?"

"Wherever you're comfortable with starting."

Haltingly, she searched for answers as she laid bare her fears and failures.

"I don't remember exactly when Malcolm began his verbal abuse. Maybe after the first failed fertility treatments? It could have been earlier, back when he started taking regular trips to Brisbane."

"What do you remember about those trips?" Graham applied a salve over each wrist and then, having ripped off the packaging of two light bandages, began carefully wrapping each wrist.

"Not much. At first the trips were infrequent. He claimed to be visiting an old school friend who wasn't well. Of course I believed him. Later I wondered if he—"

"Did you think he was seeing someone?"

She nodded. "I thought he might be visiting brothels. There was a stink of stale perfume and smoke in his clothes when I put them in the washing machine."

That had made her feel even less of a woman. And then he started undermining what little confidence she still had.

"Some men don't know when they already have a good woman in their life. He didn't deserve you." Graham placed a piece of tape on the bandage to hold the end in place and took hold of her hands again. "He's a fool, Janice, and you're well rid of him. Whatever happens, don't ever forget he deserves every day behind bars for what he did to you."

Tears pricked her eyes. She blinked, refusing to let them fall, and worked on showing Graham her only-slightly wonky smile. "You won't find me shedding any tears over his fate. Thanks for tending my wounds."

"I'm sorry you suffered at his hands."

She wriggled off the tailgate and stood. "Why are you apologising? You didn't tie me up and you've never said a cross word to me."

A muscle jumped in his cheek. "I don't expect that worm will ever give you the apology you should have."

"No. I believe you might be right."

Out of the corner of her eye she saw Graham's hand rise towards her cheek.

Excitement fluttered like a bright butterfly in her stomach. Excitement. Need. *Desire?*

His hand paused, close enough that she felt the warmth of him on her skin, and her breath caught in her throat.

She turned towards his hand.

It dropped without making contact.

The idea of tipping her cheek into his hand, of feeling his touch on her face had felt right. Bereft of a touch she had barely known she longed to feel, regret sliced through her as she sat again.

Why hadn't he touched her?

Graham busied himself with sorting through the first aid kit. "I still need to clean your bullet wound and replace that strip of your nightie with a proper bandage."

What the hell had he been thinking? He had no right to touch her. No right to care for her. She got shot on his watch.

For God's sake, how could he have put her in danger like that?

A lump of self-disgust and what might have been regret lodged in his throat. Avoiding eye contact, he took hold of her ankle and set her foot on his thigh. Her bare foot on his thigh trembled—*with pain?* Gently he unwrapped the temporary bandage. This was a whole new level of torture.

He lifted the inadequate, blood-soaked padding. Fresh blood welled in the wound and slowly dripped—one drop at a time—onto the ground. "I'll pad this more firmly and use an elastic bandage. First chance we get I'm taking you to the doctor."

"Compared to my wrists, this is a mere scratch."

"You were shot, Janice. I know how painful a gunshot wound can be so don't try to con me it isn't bothering you."

"Were you shot, Graham? Is that how you know it's painful?"

"Hmpf."

Did she imagine he'd share the horrors of that tour of duty with her?

"That's not an answer."

"Yes, I was, but I'm not going to talk about it." Concentrating on cleaning, padding, and bandaging her calf was all that stood between him and the darkness of that memory.

*The dragon is flexing his claws, spreading his wings . . .*

A soft cracking of twigs sent Graham into defence mode. He grabbed the handgun and shielded Janice with his body, ears and eyes straining to discern where the danger came from.

A moment later, a passable attempt at the call of a mopoke floated on the night air, heralding Jack's arrival. He appeared like a wraith from the trees. "It's Jack. Have you got—?"

Graham released a slow breath, put the safety on and tucked the gun into the back of his trousers, within easy reach. "Janice is safe—now."

"Top job." Jack slapped a manila folder down beside Janice and leaned against his vehicle. "There're a couple of unsavoury characters in there with Lehman. They stayed out of sight in the kitchen until I asked for a witness to sign the costs agreement."

Jack kept his voice low, but the edge of excitement was clear. Graham suspected Jack craved more adventure than what his job offered.

"Did you just happen to have the document with you?"

"I printed off a copy before I left work. It was in my briefcase in the car ready for the morning."

Janice frowned. "I didn't think you needed a witness to that sort of document."

Jack grinned. "You don't, and I won't be taking Malcolm Lehman on as a client, but hey, I thought a signature might give Smithy a name to work with. Speaking of whom, I got a text. He scrambled a team and flew out from Brisbane. Should be here within the hour."

"Good. Stay here with Janice. I want to scout the area for that second gunman."

Jack's expression changed. "One headed in the direction of the house about half a kilometre back towards town and I saw one head out this way. Lucky you didn't encounter him."

"We did." Graham took out the gun and checked the magazine.

"What?"

"I took this from him. He's tied up over there." He jerked his thumb in the direction of their prisoner. "Keep an eye on him. I won't be long."

"Graham?" Janice's soft call stopped him. He turned and

looked as she lifted one hand.

"Take my phone in case Jack needs to get in touch with you." She held out her phone.

"Good idea, Graham. I'll message you when Smithy lets me know they've landed."

Two sets of eyes looked at him expectantly.

An argument over taking the phone would delay his escape.

*Escape? Not going there.*

"Okay." He took Janice's phone, shoved it in his shirt pocket and buttoned the flap. "No lights and get Janice back inside the car."

He melted into the darkness and began the first of several sweeps around the area, feeling marginally better to be doing something to protect Janice. He might not have night vision goggles, but his night vision was still good, and his tracking skills were up to par.

But as he began his second sweep near the car, he couldn't stop thinking.

*What the hell did I think I needed to escape from?*

Susanne Bellamy

**Chapter 25**

Smithy held out a hand and Graham shook it. "Good to see you again, Graham, although I didn't expect it to be so soon. Jack said you've done a reccy. What can you tell my men?"

"I've made three sweeps around this area and Janice's house looking for the second gunman. He's returned inside with three other men. One is Malcolm Lehman, Janice's ex-husband. The other three are armed. Handguns only as far as I could see."

"Any idea what they're doing here?"

"Have you spoken to Janice yet?"

"No. Why?"

"Lehman was holding her hostage. She inherited some money. He got wind of it. She thinks he's desperate for a large sum. What little I overheard before we escaped from her house, I think they're here to collect payment."

"So he offered up his ex-wife to get out of a bind?"

"Looks like it. Doesn't matter why. The fact is, he tied her to her bed and was holding her prisoner."

Smithy signalled for the leader of the assault team to join them. "We'll get into that later. This is Jensen."

Graham nodded to the leader of the assault team.

Jensen was brief. "What's the best point of entry to that building?"

"Back door leads into the laundry, which leads into the kitchen. Wide opening into the lounge area." Graham accepted a notepad and pen from Smithy and sketched the layout of the house. "Here at the rear your men will have cover from the rainwater tank and garden shed to within ten metres of the back door. Front approach is open to a casual glance through the loungeroom windows and there's a security sensor light. The bedroom window we got out through avoids the sensor. Provided no one is using the room, I'd suggest that for the second team."

Smithy looked at the plan and tapped the front door. "Do you have a sharpshooter in the team to take out the sensor. I'd like a frontal assault in combination with that rear entry."

Graham eyed off the distance to the front veranda. "I can take that shot."

Jensen glanced at Smithy, who nodded.

"He's ex-SAS."

"I'll get you a rifle with a night scope." He left and joined his team.

Graham imagined the briefing that was taking place a hundred metres away down the lane.

He shouldn't have jumped in like that. Teams needed a clear chain of command, not outsiders pushing their way in.

But it was too late to worry about that now. And it made him feel like he was doing his part, even if nothing would ease his guilt over letting Janice get shot.

When the rifle arrived, Graham checked the magazine and then slipped through the bushes to a point with an unobstructed view of the front of the house. He positioned himself and lined up his shot. The rifle became an extension of his arm and his eyes. He breathed in and out, and then squeezed the trigger.

From this distance there was no sound of breaking glass, but a few seconds later the front door opened and one of the men stepped onto the veranda, gun at the ready. Graham watched through the scope as he stood on the edge of the veranda and looked around the yard, and then peered down the road towards town.

A second man stood in the doorway, mouthing words unheard at this distance, and the first shook his head. Both went back into the house and the door closed.

The assault team silently knelt or dropped to the ground around Graham. Jensen was beside him. "Nice shot. We'll take it from here."

"Yes, sir."

Swift and silent, dark-suited figures split into two groups and moved forward. Graham watched the mission through the night scope. Three men slipped into the rear of the yard, quickly disappearing behind the rainwater tank.

The second group of four hugged the brick façade of the front. The leader peered into the front bedroom, signalled the last member of his group to remain by the window and led the other two onto the veranda.

Graham could imagine the checking of watches, the mental countdown.

The front door was kicked in.

Light spilled onto the veranda. Voices yelled orders. Guns were trained on those inside.

Movement at the bedroom window. A man climbed through the window, landed and turned.

*Lehman.*

Graham reloaded the rifle.

*You're not getting away.*

Before he could release a warning shot the team member who had remained behind from the main assault rose from the shelter of Janice's azaleas, his gun trained on the would-be escapee.

Lehman threw his hands in the air.

Three men, hands clasped on top of their heads, were shepherded out the front door onto the veranda, followed by the team who'd entered via the laundry. Lehman was marched through the garden and joined them. Armed officers stood at front and back of them, guns levelled on the group.

Jack came to stand beside Graham. "A resounding success by the looks of it. Smithy's rubbing his hands in glee."

"Good, great." Graham disarmed his rifle and stood.

"How's Janice?"

"Holding up, but she looks exhausted."

"I want to get her to the doctor's as soon as possible. Can you drive us there?"

"Sure. I'll clear it with Smithy. Looks like you might not have to go into hiding any longer if what Smithy suspects is true."

"What's that?"

"That they've caught the new boss of Hickman's gang."

Susanne Bellamy

**Chapter 26**

Graham sat on the steps of the police station and took the last cup of coffee from a cardboard tray proffered by Darcy Carmichael. The red-haired owner of the bakery café had arrived with the tray of coffees and taken them straight inside. "Thanks, but who ordered the coffee?"

Darcy's smile didn't reach her eyes. "Jack. He always orders a delivery when he's called to the police station to see a client. He says he can't think clearly so early in the morning without caffeine."

"We all pulled an all-nighter. Could you bring another round up later? On me." He took out his wallet and handed over a note. "Keep the change."

"Sure, thanks." Darcy glanced at the front door of the station and Graham finally identified the emotion flickering through her eyes. Worry.

"Is Janice okay? I don't mean to pry, but I heard she'd been shot."

"She was. Only superficial, but even those sting. The doctor's dressing the wound now, but she's fine, Darcy."

"That's a relief. Tell her I said hello. I'll be back in an hour or so with your coffees." This time her smile lit her face and the blue of her eyes was like a summer sky. She walked down the path and turned left at the gate, striding down the footpath.

It was strange to be connecting close enough with people that he knew the colour of their eyes. From O'Reilly's Ridge, he could tell the identity of a person from their gait, but the close-up details had eluded him.

He'd never let anyone get close before Rick. And then Gei, and Anna and Jack. Kaden. Even Smithy.

The list was longer than he could ever have imagined. People he knew. People he liked. People he was comfortable being around.

*And now Janice . . .*

He waited for the familiar clenching in his gut; the tension that came with thinking about being in a group of people.

There was definitely a twinge, but the mind-numbing fear was no longer in the forefront of his mind.

Exposure therapy, Rick said. Maybe there was something in it.

The interview room at the police station had been taken over by Smithy and his team. Two of his men were currently interviewing Lex Porter, formerly the second-in-command and now *the boss*. He'd escaped the round up of most of Hickman's gang last year.

How much of Hickman's operation had Porter taken over? And how did the stuff he'd dug up with Jack fit into the picture?

The front door opened and Jack joined Graham on the top

step, a cup of Darcy's coffee in his hand. "The prisoners will be transferred to Brisbane this afternoon. The facilities here aren't big enough to keep them separate and Lehman's whining the others will kill him if he's put in a cell with them."

"Good riddance." Feeling charitable towards that worm was beyond Graham. "Does Smithy need me for anything else or can I go?"

Smithy's voice followed the squeak of the front door opening. "Graham, one more favour to ask. Can you show two of my men where you found the toolbox folder?"

"I can. Now?"

"In a couple of hours. Porter's trying to trade off information in the hope of reducing his sentence later. He's given us the information that, from jail, Hickman arranged for evidence of his criminal activities to be buried on that land between the ridge and Jack's cottage. He figured there was no connection between him and that land."

"Do you mean there's more buried in the meadow?" Graham shook his head. How had he missed seeing the signs of that disturbance?

"Apparently. The man he entrusted with that task was picked up by police soon after, got into a fight in jail and took a bad beating. He's still in a coma and the doctors believe his brain damage is so severe, he'll have no memory of anything."

"I'm guessing no one else knows the location and Porter

was prepared to dig up the whole area to reclaim the evidence. What about the stuff Jack and I dug up?"

"Porter's insurance in case anything happened to him. The financial papers alone are enough to put Hickman away until he's a very old man."

"And Fiesta Holdings? What has that got to do with the surveyors' markers?"

Smithy leaned one shoulder against the wall and crossed his ankles. "It's a shelf company created for the sole purpose of acquiring the land so no one would find what was buried there."

Jack patted Graham's shoulder and raised his coffee cup in a toast. "Looks like you're free and clear to go on living on the ridge."

Graham frowned and rubbed his stubbled chin. "Maybe, but it's been a wake-up call for me. Can you look into that squatter's rights aspect and see if I have a claim?"

"I can do that. I've already researched Queensland law regarding adverse possession, and I think we can make a strong case."

"I hate to interrupt your legal consultation, but can we come back to the current case?" Smithy's dry manner brought both Graham and Jack's attention back. "About Janice."

Graham frowned. How could he have forgotten her, even for a minute?

"She's still in the doctor's surgery."

"We've barely touched on the murder, but we do know the dead man was Lehman's business partner, Michael de Leno. They got into a bad situation and borrowed heavily from Hickman's loan shark. De Leno had no hope of repaying the loan, but Lehman found out by chance about Janice's inheritance. He saved his skin by telling them he could lay his hands on a lot of money if he could establish renewed relationship and co-habitation with her."

Jack got to his feet, walked a little way down the path and turned to face them. "I get it now. They killed de Leno to make Lehman hurry things along with Janice."

Gut churning, Graham also stood. "And Janice refused to have a bar of him. He got desperate when he saw the police poster of his dead business partner."

Smithy nodded. "Which is why he resorted to holding her hostage."

"Is there any sort of counselling you can access for Janice?" Graham might not have sought counselling for himself, but Janice deserved whatever assistance was available.

"Some for victims of crime; but compensation is minimal. The problem is what to do for her in the short term following her ordeal. I've had a crime trauma counsellor on the phone. She suggests Janice will be better if she can stay with someone she trusts away from where she was held hostage. You, Graham, more than anyone, will understand the feelings she'll be experiencing."

"You're asking me to look after her?"

"Nobody better." Smithy's gaze narrowed, hitting Graham like a laser-beam.

"She got shot because I made a bad decision. I should have made a different choice. Why would she trust me now?"

"It's not the usual witness protection assignment, but I understand you and she are close?"

"Not exactly." But before Janice had been taken hostage, he'd almost dared to hope they could have been.

"And where do you think I should take a traumatised woman? Up to my tent on the ridge?"

"Hmm, see what you can find. You've got permission to access her house for the purpose of collecting clothing for the short term."

One of his team asked Smithy to return to the interview room.

Smithy pinned Graham with a look that saw through his half-hearted excuse and unsettled him.

Was this a test of his fitness to participate in the witness protection program? How much of his background did Smithy know?

Damn it, he had to man up. He'd do better this time.

"Consider it done. Maybe the shearers' quarters behind the winery will do for a night or two. I'll ask Rick."

Smithy nodded and disappeared back inside.

"Can I borrow your phone and your car, Jack?"

Jack handed his keys and phone to Graham and stood, stretching his arms over his head. "I'd better get back in there. Drop them at the front counter when you finish. No rest for the wicked, hey, Graham?"

"You've got that right."

A short phone call later, Rick had promised a shearer's room would be ready for Janice whenever Graham arrived.

Janice valued her independence. What would she think of these arrangements being made for her?

He stood, drained the coffee and tossed the cup into the bin on the footpath. How best to present the decisions that had been made on her behalf to Janice? The problem occupied him as he crossed the road and paused outside the front door.

The surgery was busy when Graham stepped through the door. Heads turned, magazines and phones were lowered. Nine pairs of eyes settled on him and prickles of discomfort pierced his skin.

*I can do this.*

Three strides carried him to the front counter where Dora Romney sat in front of a computer screen.

She glanced up and smiled. "Hello, Graham. Are you here to collect Janice?"

He nodded, swallowed, pushed out a single word. "Yes."

"Come through please." She led the way down a hall to the last room on the right and knocked gently before opening the door.

"Graham's here when you've finished with Ms Lehman, Dr Manning."

"He can come in now. I've finished dressing the wounds."

Dora pushed the door wide and stood to one side. "I've done the online forms, Janice, so you can slip out the back door rather than come back through the waiting room."

"Thanks, Dora. I'm grateful to escape appearing in public dressed like this."

Graham stood in the doorway, uncertain about stepping into the room.

*I've no right to be here. I failed to protect her when it mattered. Why does Smithy think my presence will reassure her after that?*

Janice was sitting on the examination table. Her dressing gown was ripped and dirty and her feet were bare, her hair was a bird's nest, but she looked at him and smiled. "I'm ready to go home."

She smiled like she was really pleased to see him. How could that be?

He cleared his throat, the *ahem* soft, but audible. "Right. Jack's loaned us his car."

Dr Manning offered her arm to Janice to climb off the table. "Rest that leg for the next day or two, and no heavy lifting until your wrists have healed. I'd like to see you in a week." The doctor met Graham's gaze. "You did a fine job of dressing Janice's wounds. Change the dressings daily to begin with. I've given Janice a prescription for antibiotic cream."

"Will do."

He held out his arm for Janice to lean on if she chose. When her hand wrapped around his arm, he felt the weight of her fatigue in her tight grip. They took the short ramp at the rear of the building slowly and ambled down the side path, brushing past overhanging branches and the glossy dark-green leaves of overhanging cliveas. In summer the pathway would be cool and pleasant, but Janice shivered and gripped her dressing gown under her chin.

"Nearly there. Just the road to cross and then I'll go to the pharmacy."

Janice tugged on his arm before they rounded the corner into full view of the street. "Would you mind bringing the car as close as possible please?"

"This walking is too much for you. I can carry you across—"

"No, Graham, it isn't my leg so much, although it's sore, but I don't want to be seen in public like this."

"Ah, right." He left her hanging onto the corner of the building and jogged across the road to where Jack's vehicle was parked in front of the police station. In a single smooth manoeuvre, he reversed out of the parking bay and back across the road into the brick paved area at the front of the surgery.

Janice was limping towards the front passenger door before he got out and could reach her.

He opened the door and helped her in. "Do you want to sit in the car here, or in front of the pharmacy?"

"The pharmacy if you don't mind, Graham. I feel more exposed here."

He closed her door and drove the short distance to the pharmacy.

He was served quickly and had the supplies in a paper bag tucked under his arm and was heading to the front door when the sweet, spicy scent of a bucket of carnations stopped him.

Dithering about the purchase, he glanced into Jack's car. Janice's eyes were closed, her arms folded tightly across her chest.

Making a snap decision, Graham bought a bunch of pink and yellow carnations and returned to the car.

Janice opened her eyes as he climbed in, her eyes widening as he handed the bunch of flowers to her.

"Thank you, Graham. They're lovely."

Janice buried her nose in the perfumed carnations. She wanted to tell Graham what his gift meant to her, but his gruff voice and stern profile dissuaded her from further conversation even after he turned onto her road.

As they crested the rise and her house came into view, collywobbles began jiggling in her stomach. Clutching the flowers to her chest she tried to slow her breathing and control the racing of her heart.

But the closer they came, the harder it was to draw breath into her tight lungs.

She'd tried to make the rental house a home, tried to be happy there as she teetered at the beginning of a life without Malcolm in it.

And then he'd come into her house, invaded her life and turned it upside down.

*I can't stay there.*

She'd see him every time she looked at the sofa, every time she walked into the kitchen. And the bedroom . . .

Shudders rippled down her spine.

Graham turned into the driveway and pulled up behind her vehicle. He switched off the engine and sat, hands on the wheel and looking at her house.

Crime scene tape fluttered across the front door. The side of one of the azalea bushes drooped, the broken branches beginning to show signs of dying. *All those boots,* she thought.

"You don't have to go inside, Janice."

Such a gentle voice Graham had. She could listen to him all day.

"I have to face up to the mess sometime. Best done sooner than later." Her clenching stomach disagreed. If there were any way to avoid going inside now, the old Janice would take it.

Not the new Janice. She was going to face up to her problems and deal with them. God knew how she'd sleep here though.

"This is home. I'll make the best of it until I can find somewhere else to live."

Except it would never feel like home again. Not when the mere thought of going into her bedroom sent a rush of blood to her head.

"About that. Your house is a crime scene. Smithy said the trauma counsellor suggested you stay elsewhere for the time being, but he's given permission to enter your house so you can pack a bag for a short-term absence."

"Oh." Who could she stay with? "Katy might have a room at her B and B, or Moira might be able to—"

"Rick and Gei have offered you the shearers' quarters. Probably should have started with that."

Relief coursed through her. "That could work."

"After Rick stayed there when he first started working for the Romneys, they installed hot water and an indoor shower. It's still basic, but—"

"No, it sounds good. I don't think I could have faced staying here by myself after . . ." She sucked in a quick breath. "Sorry. I'm being a wuss."

"You're not. Nobody likes being reminded of bad things. Do you want me to pack that bag for you?"

"You know what? Knowing I don't have to sleep here makes me feel a lot better. I'll come in and pack." She put the flowers on the floor and opened the door.

Graham was beside her, his arm at the ready before she manoeuvred her bound leg outside. "Try not to touch anything inside that you don't need."

"In and out in as short a time as possible suits me." She took his arm and limped beside him around the back of her vehicle.

Shattered glass littered the front steps and path. She glanced up. The sensor light was broken. "Looks like Malcolm's pals were pretty rough."

"The broken light was my fault. I shot it."

"From where we were last night? That's impressive." Considering the distance and the darkness, Graham must be a fine shot. It was another reminder of his military past. "So what did the light do to you?"

"Was that a joke?"

"Pathetic attempt, I know."

"Pretty good under the circumstances." Graham lifted the police tape and pushed the front door open.

Janice ducked under his arm. "They didn't lock up?"

"Lock's broken. That wasn't me. Smithy's team came in a two-pronged attack front and rear. They kicked the doors open."

Muddy boot prints tracked through from the laundry and kitchen and across the pale grey carpet, looking like a weird post-modern work of art. She'd never liked that style of art.

"Where's your suitcase?"

"There're two in the hallway linen cupboard. How long does Smithy think I'll need to pack for?"

"He didn't say. Pack all your clothes if you want."

"Maybe I will. I'll be happy if I don't ever have to come back here."

Graham took her hand and, for the first time since he'd picked her up at the doctor's, made deliberate eye contact. There was sympathy and understanding in his gaze. "You don't have to come back. When you decide where you want to live, I can pack up the house for you. You'll never have to set foot inside again, if you don't want to."

He led her down the hall and opened the door into her bedroom. One arm rested across her shoulders and he kept hold of her hand and drew her into the room.

Cut ropes lay where they'd fallen on the floor.

She gasped. Recoiled.

Graham pulled her closer. "You never have to come back in here after today but face it down now. Replace it with one final memory that isn't about pain and fear. Look at it, remember the good and replace the bad memories with something positive."

She nodded, turned to him and met his eyes. Dark brown eyes that had looked at her as a woman and not as a chattel. Eyes she wanted to look into across the breakfast table in the morning;

in her bed last thing at night.

*I know what I want to remember.*

She set a hand on Graham's cheek and tipped her face up.

Slowly, shyly, she touched her lips to his.

Several heartbeats passed in this lightest of kisses. Heartbeats in which she feared she'd misread sympathy for something more than simple friendship.

Breaking contact would mean facing him, facing up to another rejection.

And that would be her fault.

Graham let go of her hand.

She drew back to end the kiss, but Graham slid his hand into her hair and suddenly he was kissing her like there was no tomorrow.

This was a kiss to weave a dream on. A kiss to chase away her nightmare memories and build a future around.

But then Graham groaned, released her and stepped back. "I'm sorry, Janice. I shouldn't have done that."

"What—kiss me back? You didn't start it. I did. And I enjoyed it, very much."

He looked at the floor, at the bed, and closed his eyes for a moment before turning away. "I'll get your suitcases."

Susanne Bellamy

## Chapter 27

Graham pushed open the door of the easternmost room of the shearers' quarters and set Janice's suitcases down on one of the lower bunk beds. He looked around the room Rick had lived in when he started work at the winery and cringed.

Dark wooden walls leached the light from the space. Two narrow windows with unbleached cotton curtains—the curtains, an addition since Rick lived here. A single strip fluorescent tube hung over a plain wooden table and two bench seats. He flicked the light switch on, desperate for lighting to somehow magically make the room look better.

In the far corner, another curtain separated the living space from the recently added shower and toilet.

His heart sank.

*What made me think this would do for Janice? Why didn't I go along with her suggestion of a room at the B and B?*

Rick and Gei had made this room as welcoming as it could be. A small vase of flowers from the home garden sat on a scratched bedside table, and a picnic hamper sat on the end of the table. A bright yellow tablecloth covered the table, but none of the touches could disguise how basic the room was. This wasn't what Janice deserved.

*And I sure as hell can't offer her better. A tent on a*

*mountain with no running water.*

Janice followed him in and, sitting on a bench, opened the hamper and peered inside. "How kind of Rick and Gei to send over some food."

"Gei's thoughtful like that."

He dragged in a deep breath and faced her. "I'm sorry, Janice. I don't know what I was thinking. You need better and warmer rooms. I'll take you to Katy's B and B and see if—"

"Graham Peyton, just how much of a princess do you think I am?"

"What?"

"This is simple, I agree, but it's clean, there's a bed, food, hot water, privacy. What more could I ask for?"

The strip fluoro bathed the room in white light that highlighted its deficiencies.

"A heater? Better lighting? People around you?"

"Right now, I have everything I need right here." Her gaze settled on him and her lips parted.

Such a small action, one he wouldn't have noticed before he kissed her.

But he had and now he wanted to go on kissing her. He wanted what he had no right to want.

*What the hell was I thinking kissing her like that?*

The kiss had played on his mind as he fetched and carried, helping her to pack her entire wardrobe of clothes, the contents of her chest of drawers and fill a black, heavy-duty garbage bag full of shoes.

And sheets, towels, pillows . . . everything but the kitchen sink.

He'd carried everything to Jack's SUV and stowed it in the boot, and when he'd come back inside and stuck his head around the bedroom door to ask if there was anything else she wanted, she was in the shower.

The door was closed, but it changed his memory of that kiss. It built a need he'd subdued for too long as he imagined kissing her in the shower.

"Graham?"

"Sorry. What?" Think of anything else. Think of waking the bees. Think of their stings when their hive was knocked over.

"Will you stay with me tonight?"

"Of course. I'll be in the adjoining room. Or maybe across your doorway. I haven't decided."

Her frown told him he'd got it wrong.

"Graham, I'd like it if you stayed in here. With me."

"I don't need to be inside to keep you safe. Malcolm can't hurt you anymore."

There was a long pause. Her frown deepened as she skated on the edge of understanding what he was saying.

"Smithy asked me to keep an eye on you. That's why I brought you here. I can do my job better out here than in town."

"Better as in, you don't like being inside buildings or because it's easier to get back to your home on the hill from here?"

Janice's cheeks pinked up and she sat straighter. Linking her fingers on the table, she pinned him with a direct look, a look that demanded the truth. "So you wouldn't have stayed around if I wasn't your *job*?"

Words had power. Graham knew.

Only this time, there were no good words. No right and fitting words.

He was damned if he agreed with her and doing wrong by her if he didn't.

Because no matter how much he wanted to stay, he hadn't protected her when she needed him. But he'd do all he could to protect her now.

He wouldn't let down another woman he liked—*maybe even—loved?*

"I'll check in on you later." He pulled the door closed behind him.

Hours later Janice woke, curled up in a ball of misery under her doona. She'd slept the deep sleep of the emotionally exhausted.

Waking was no picnic. Doubts and fears flowed back as she looked around the room.

It was truly mortifying. Kissing Graham, asking him to stay—inviting him into her bed and having him refuse.

How could she have misread that kiss?

Now, lying on the bunk bed watching sunbeams dance on the wall in the late afternoon light, it was past time to make some tough decisions.

As much as she loved Lark Creek, maybe it was time to leave.

A quiet knock at the door encouraged her to sit up and run her hands over her bed hair before calling, "Come in."

Gei Romney entered and set a covered pie dish on the table. "Hi, Janice. I hope I didn't wake you. I just wanted to make sure you've got everything you need and to leave this. Apple pie."

Janice relaxed. She'd expected her caller to be Graham, but right now, while she was feeling vulnerable and at sea, he was the last person she wanted to see. "I've got all I need, and thanks for the pie. It was kind of you and Rick to let me stay here."

"I thought you'd prefer a room in our home, but Graham struggles with being inside and he refused to leave you."

"This room is fine, and it's only for a few days, although I have no desire to return to the house I was in. But you know, Graham doesn't need to babysit me. I'm sure he's champing at the bit to get back up to his precious ridge."

Gei tipped her head and her eyes narrowed as she looked at the closed door and back to Janice. "Is that what you think, that Graham considers you a burden?"

"He told me I'm his *assignment*."

"Did he?"

"Well, as good as. Maybe not in so many words."

"He's a good man, Janice, but he struggles with things most of us can't begin to imagine. Rick thinks that he's made progress recently."

"What sort of progress? Do you mean his claustrophobia?"

"That and other things. When you were ill, he spent more time inside in one night than he's managed in a year of visiting us for dinner. We've sat outside drinking coffee when the thermometer was close to zero because of his phobia. It's my belief he's finally found someone he wants to make the effort for."

"Rick. Discovering he has a son must have been wonderful."

"Connecting with Rick was huge, but it was only the first step. Oh, don't get me wrong. It's wonderful for both of them. But while family is important, it's just one sort of relationship. Graham's discovered another that's inspired him."

"You can't mean me. We're friends, sort of. At least I thought we were. But he's been distant since . . ." Janice stopped. Thought.

When did Graham start keeping his distance? Not when they were trapped in the roof. She felt like they were close, and she'd helped him stay calm. But afterwards . . .

She wrapped her arms around her knees and stroked a patch of bright blue silk in her doona. "After we escaped, when he was taping my bullet wound—he behaved strangely. And today it's as if—"

Was it possible he felt partly responsible for her being shot? But that was ridiculous.

Feeling the prick of tears, she turned her head and looked through the window. The view blurred, colours smudging into one another. "I like watching the light changing outside. It turns the trunks of the ghost gums golden."

"Janice, you know everyone's worrying about you. They can't believe you got shot. But I think Graham's taking it harder than anyone. He's a protector, and he cares for you."

She sniffed, swallowed, and took a deep breath. "I'm starting to see how that might be."

"I'm glad you are. And now I'd better get back to the house. Rick will be home soon."

Janice turned and squeezed her hand. "Gei, thank you."

As soon as Gei left, Janice went into the tiny bathroom and splashed water on her face. Her knee-jerk reaction, thinking she should leave Lark Creek, was only one option.

*Do I really want to go? What Gei suggested changes everything.*

A gentle knocking tapped before her front door opened. "Janice, it's Graham. Are you okay?" He sounded worried. "I saw Gei leaving. Did you need something?"

Holding back the curtain, she stood in the doorway. "I'm

fine, physically."

"And mentally? I know how an experience like you suffered plays over and over in the mind. I was talking to Jack about you seeing someone, a psychologist. He's found someone he's started seeing and can recommend." He stood in the doorway, holding the doorknob in one hand and the doorjamb in the other.

"Arranging my life again, were you, Graham?"

"I—ah—" He frowned.

*Why won't he come in?*

*He's in no man's land.*

The strange description popped into Janice's head in a light bulb moment. *No man's land—meaning: unoccupied due to fear or uncertainty.*

*Is that how Graham sees stepping into a room? As a fearful experience?*

"Tell me, who did you talk to when you came back from your war? Who helped you deal with your experiences?"

He shook his head. "No one."

"Are you telling me you retreated to O'Reilly's Ridge all alone and stayed there for thirty years? Without talking to anyone. In heaven's name, why?"

"I don't talk about—"

"Don't you dare say you won't talk about your experience and in the next breath try to tell me I should talk to someone about mine. If it's good enough for me then it's good enough for you.

We're going to start right now. Come in and sit down, Graham. And then tell me about being trapped in the roof with me."

Graham eyed off the room. Four walls. One door. No escape.

He didn't want to take that final step into the room and into this conversation with Janice.

He'd been in other rooms before and he could do it without the full panic response exploding in his brain.

But not this time.

Not when the woman he had feelings for sat on the bench and looked expectantly at him.

If he went into the room, if he opened his big mouth and told her about his fears—*if I expose the real me*—

"Come on, Graham. You've been inside lots of times. There's nothing different about this time."

*The hell there's not.*

"You want me to come inside, into a confined space where I'm trapped, and talk about *my feelings*? Not happening."

"I'm no psychologist, but your reluctance sounds like you're afraid of me. That can't be right, not after—all we've been through together."

"Say what you were going to. Not after I kissed you."

"Graham, you turned my bedroom, a place that was awful, into a memory I'll treasure for the rest of my life. But I'll come back to that later. This is about you and how you saved me."

"Saved you? You got shot because of the decisions I made. If I'd chosen a better option, you wouldn't have suffered that bullet wound."

"That's one way of looking at it, although I believe you're seeing it the wrong way around."

"There is no other way of looking at it."

"Did you expect some arachnophobic criminal to shoot a spider in my bedroom?"

"No, but—"

"No, of course not." Janice set both hands on the table, palms down and met his gaze. "If you hadn't chosen to go into the roof, where else could we have gone?"

"Through the window wasn't possible. Hickman's men had arrived, and one stayed with the car. He'd have seen us if we'd gone that way." By himself he might have risked that exit, risked the bullets, but not with Janice.

She nodded, her gaze holding his, refusing to let him off the hook. "Any other choices?"

"We could have gone down the hall and out through the second bedroom."

"Risking being seen or heard by Malcolm or his visitors. We didn't—what's that army phrase?"

"Have eyes on them?"

"That's the one. We had no idea if anyone was standing

outside the bedroom, or in the hall where they could see us as soon as we opened the door. Was there another choice?"

"No."

"So your decision to go up was a good one."

"Maybe."

"It was the only possible choice. Moving on. I'm aware you experienced some *discomfort* being in a dark, confined space with me, but was there anything positive that came out of that?"

Janice being there.

She talked, and kept him calm. And he was happy she let him hold her when she was scared. Her body tucked in beside his, her warm and soothing voice keeping his dragon at bay—they were positives.

Janice watched him, clearly waiting for some response.

Reluctantly he admitted, "I didn't go ballistic in the confined space."

She nodded. "I noticed that. Why do you think that was?"

"I don't know."

How could he tell her she was the reason?

"Hmm, I think you do, and I think you're more scared of telling me the real reason why you managed that stressful situation."

"Janice, please. Let it go." His chest was tight, his grip on the door, deathly. He shook his head. "Just—drop it."

"I don't think so. What was the difference?"

Closing his eyes, he dragged in an audible breath, releasing it in a rush of words.

"Dammit, you, Janice. You were the difference this time."

"This time?" Soft, careful, seeking answers but not pushing him now, Janice's voice drew him into the room. "I'm here if you want to tell me about the other time."

One step. Two. A third brought him to the table.

Janice tipped her head up.

In her eyes he saw no pity. Just compassion, and an invitation to share.

He slumped on the bench, glanced at her, dragged his gaze away. But there was something about Janice that he couldn't resist. He met her eyes, her soft, brown, understanding eyes.

Could he tell her?

Bare bones only.

Looking at the table, he uttered words he'd never shared, never imagined he could share, with anyone.

"We were on routine patrol in a small town when we got wind of a trap. A woman came towards our vehicle."

*A woman in a blue dupatta. I watched her come through the sight on my rifle.*

"It looked like she wanted help, but she was wired up—a suicide bomber. The bomb detonated and killed three of my men; one of them was our driver. The vehicle was damaged in the blast so the rest of us raced into a building. We holed up there while a barrage of shells hit the area. The building took a direct hit. It killed the rest of my unit. I was buried alive for two days."

*With a dead body and a beam pinning me down, but that's not for Janice's ears.*

She covered his hand with both of hers. The simple touch was comforting, steadying. It brought him out of that collapsed cellar and back into the shearer's room. It anchored him in the here and now and refused to let the darkness claim him.

"I'm here, Graham. Thank you for trusting me enough to share what happened to you."

Sharing that nightmare—even the sanitised version of it—lifted the weight of survivor guilt from his shoulders.

*I survived and my mates were all killed. I've never dealt with that. I hid on the ridge and I wasn't there for Rick and Alice. But maybe if I talk to a psych, I can be here for Janice.*

"You're right about the psychiatrist. I should have gone years ago. I might not have stuffed up Alice and Rick's lives if I'd talked about it."

"It takes courage to do what you've done, to find a path you can walk. And Graham—" She waited, stroking his hands until their gazes connected and held.

He shook his head. "I'm not brave. I've lived with this fear of being trapped for so long I doubt I could ever live inside a house."

"What about a house with big windows? We could build

something that brings the outdoors inside."

He frowned. "What do you mean *we can build*? Don't you think less of me because of my weakness?"

"Graham Peyton, that had better be the last time you utter such nonsense. I've never known a stronger or more caring man. You charged into the lion's den to rescue me and faced your worst nightmare to keep me safe.

"You dwell on your fear as a weakness, but I see a man who fights harder than anyone I've ever known. I admire and respect you and I would like it if you might consider—if you'd think about taking a chance—on me?"

Wonder filled him. Wonder and awe and hope. Janice knew his worst fears and still she wanted to be with him.

*And I want to be with Janice.*

"A second chance for both of us. I like it. But let's take it one day at a time for now. Sort out this thing with your ex and the Hickman gang, and find out what's happening with the surveyor's pegs?"

"That's a good idea."

"Jack thinks I may have a claim to land near my winter campsite." He looked at her and somehow the impossible had become entirely probable.

"So, it's a glass house you're wanting?" Large windows looking down the slope to Lark Creek took shape in his mind. A view framed by a home shared with the woman he was falling in love with.

Janice smiled and it was like the sun coming up on a brand new day.

"I like looking at the stars at night from my bed. And the sunrise."

Susanne Bellamy

## Chapter 28

*Six months later*

"Graham? What did that letter from Jack say? Is there any news?" Janice stopped beside the newly planted rosemary grevillea.

He set down his spade. "Come sit with me and I'll tell you." He drew her down onto the rustic log bench he'd set at the top of the meadow. Here, they sat most evenings watching the fireflies flit across the meadow as lights came on in Lark Creek.

"The best news. The court has granted my claim to a plot of land that stretches from where I planted the flowering bushes and set up the first beehives all the way down to the beehives near the creek. It goes up the ridge a little way and includes my winter campsite, with an easement for public passage through to the ridge. The judge said because I used and improved the land over so many years, she accepted my claim. I reckon it was the bees that tipped it though."

"Everything you hoped for. Well done, darling." She wrapped her arms around his neck and hugged him.

The right to love Janice had seemed like a miracle, the most wonderful gift she could have given him, and the wonder of her touch still took him by surprise.

*To touch and be touched.*

*To love and be loved.*

"Now we've got this decision we can begin breaking ground for the house as soon as you want."

"Tomorrow?"

Graham grinned and rested his head against hers. In his mind he could see a small rustic cottage with a wall of windows looking out towards the creek. "Maybe the day after. Tomorrow we're driving to the Gold Coast for that yoga class for military and first responders that you found online. But the day after, I'll wrestle with building permits for the dormitory building at the same time as for our home; do it all in one hit if I can."

"I know the grant you won allows for accommodation for up to six students and a teacher. Just—can we keep a bit of distance between our home and the school?"

"With a wall of glass, you'd better believe the students will be at a distance. When I come home at the end of the day, I don't want to share you with anyone."

Janice smiled and kissed his lips. For all that it was a quick kiss, the look in her eye promised an interesting evening. "I don't intend sharing you once you come home from work."

"I waited thirty years for you, and for this home we'll build together."

"But we are home, Graham. Home isn't just a place to lay your head. It's being with the people you love, and I do love you."

"Then welcome home, my love. I've cooked dinner for

you.”

**_The End_**

*Thank you for reading 'Home from the Hill'. Please consider leaving a review and sharing your enjoyment with other readers.*

Find out more about Susanne Bellamy and her books at
www.susannebellamy.com
Follow her on Bookbub:
https://www.bookbub.com/authors/susanne-bellamy
Facebook: https://www.facebook.com/susannebellamyauthor/

*Acknowledgements: With many thanks to my CP buddy, Shirley Wine, and to my wonderful editor, Annie Seaton.*

9 780648 527596